# The Cuffer Anthology
## VOLUME IV

### A Selection of Short Fiction from Newfoundland and Labrador

© 2012, Pam Frampton

 Canada Council for the Arts   Conseil des Arts du Canada   Canadä    Newfoundland Labrador

We gratefully acknowledge the financial support of the Canada Council for the Arts, the Government of Canada through the Canada Book Fund (CBF), and the Government of Newfoundland and Labrador through the Department of Tourism, Culture and Recreation for our publishing program.

All rights reserved. No part of this work covered by the copyrights hereon may be reproduced or used in any form or by any means—graphic, electronic or mechanical—without the prior written permission of the publisher. Any requests for photocopying, recording, taping or information storage and retrieval systems of any part of this book shall be directed in writing to the Canadian Reprography Collective, One Yonge Street, Suite 1900, Toronto, Ontario M5E 1E5.

Cover design by Todd Manning / Layout by Amy Fitzpatrick
Printed on acid-free paper

Published by
KILLICK PRESS
an imprint of CREATIVE BOOK PUBLISHING
a Transcontinental Inc. associated company
P.O. Box 8660, Stn. A
St. John's, Newfoundland and Labrador A1B 3T7

Printed in Canada by:
TRANSCONTINENTAL INC.

FSC
www.fsc.org
MIX
Paper from responsible sources
FSC® C011825

Library and Archives Canada Cataloguing in Publication

The Cuffer anthology. Volume IV : a selection of short fiction / Pam Frampton, editor.

ISBN 978-1-897174-99-9

1. Short stories, Canadian (English)--Newfoundland and Labrador.
2. Canadian fiction (English)--21st century. I. Frampton, Pam

PS8329.5.N3C834 2012      C813'.01089718      C2012-905022-9

# The Cuffer Anthology
VOLUME IV

A Selection of Short Fiction
from Newfoundland and Labrador

Edited by Pam Frampton

St. John's, Newfoundland and Labrador
2012

# INTRODUCTION

If this is your first encounter with *The Cuffer Anthology*, you are on the threshold of a very enjoyable read. Find a comfortable seat, settle in and prepare to be captivated.

*The Cuffer Anthology: Volume IV* contains 35 of the best stories from the Cuffer Prize 2011 competition. Choosing which stories made it in and which ones didn't was tough — there were so many excellent entries; so many wonderful writers whose work deserves to be showcased. Thanks to everyone who entered the competition. It was fascinating to see the world through your eyes.

The stories you'll find in these pages are all different, of course, but they have things in common, as well. They are all set in this province, and the authors have found ways to describe life here — whether set in the harsh and unforgiving coastal landscape or in the seedy underbelly of a city — with authenticity and flair.

In *Adele*, Deborah Whelan describes an evening in Tea Cove: "The world turned navy blue as they walked up the hill, the only light coming from the stars and the lamp-lit windows that stained the grass in stretched rectangles."

In *Iteration*, Annette Conway's depiction of early morning on Prescott Street will resonate with anyone who has spent any time in downtown St. John's: "When the sun rises in The Narrows, fingers of light paint the houses on Prescott Street red. ... The smell of last night's rain drifts off the pavement and she knows it will be a cool day because there is no smell of sewage drifting up from the harbour."

One entrant to the Cuffer Prize 2011 lamented the fact that the competition is limited to stories that are 1,200 words or less. The main reason is that, each year, the 10 shortlisted stories are published in The Telegram's Books section, so that they can reach a wider audience. And 1,200 words fill a newspaper page, along with an illustration. But even without that space consideration, while there are certainly plenty of fine short stories in the world that are much longer than 1,200 words, those published here are proof that sometimes less is more. It's amazing how much life and loss and happiness and heartache Cuffer Prize authors can condense into that word limit, and at how true to life their characters are, and how real the worlds they create.

In a pair of back-to-back stories written by Ed Turpin, you'll find a detailed portrait of friendship that begins in *Dinks*, with the two main characters as young boys, and continues in *Recycling*, where they are now men with half their lives behind them.

There are plenty of life lessons to be gleaned from these stories; many of the characters are captured on the page at a point where their lives have changed significantly, or are about to. There is the sorrow spawned by absence in Cuffer Prize first-place winner Grant Loveys' *Our Guys*: "Never met the fella in my life. And he smiled the way you did. Looked exactly like you for a second. It's hard to take that as just one more weird thing in a world full of them, especially now with you gone."

There is keen observation from a 12-year-old girl whose mother is dead and who feels rejected by her father, in Chad Pelley's *What the Difference Is*. She likes to hang out at the emergency department at St. Clare's Hospital, where she sees people whose lives are often worse — or at least, more interesting — than her own. Her detachment in describing the people she sees masks her own pain and sorrow. Assessing the human frailties on display she notes that: "A kid named Pete lost a chunk of his tongue on a cold bus stop pole on LeMarchant Road. ... the front part of the tongue where the 'sweet-sensing' tastebuds are. He'd lost the best part of his tongue on a dare, and now his life will be forever bitter. Or salty."

The alienation of youth is a common theme. In *Regal Hill*, Josh Pennell's protagonist struggles to match his older brothers' tough reputations in order to fit into his hardscrabble neighbourhood, but in the end finds out that being the victor in a fight is not always satisfying.

In Michael Nolan's *Miss Fyfe*, an ostentatious moniker leads to ostracism for an orphaned girl named Bertha Beryl Ling-Ling Goobie-Fyfe.

And in Joshua Goudie's disturbing but poignant *The Goat*, sexual abuse brings pain, shame and change to a young victim.

Other stories depict the simple pleasures of domesticity, the perils of living life on a downward spiral, and the bittersweet collisions that can occur when the realities of modern life intrude on simpler times.

I hope readers have the pleasure of losing themselves — temporarily — in the fascinating places these writers have given life to. I also hope that reading *The Cuffer Anthology: Volume IV* makes you want to go out and buy Volumes I, II and III if you don't own them already. Proceeds from the sale of these books go to a good cause — Literacy Newfoundland and Labrador — and you'll be giving a nod to writing talent that is certainly worth fostering.

Some of the writers featured here will be known to you already, and the ones that aren't, should be. May you enjoy their writing as much as I have, as have our Cuffer Prize judges, Ramona Dearing, Joan Sullivan and Russell Wangersky.

Thanks to them and special thanks to Todd Manning and Amy Fitzpatrick for the wonderful layout, Donna Francis and Pam Dooley of Creative Book Publishing for their unflagging enthusiasm for this project, and to my husband, Glenn Payette, for his interest and constant encouragement.

*Pam Frampton*
*St. John's*

# CUFFER PRIZE ANTHOLOGY 2012

## stories

| | |
|---|---|
| Our Guys, by Grant Loveys | 1 |
| What The Difference Is, by Chad Pelley | 5 |
| Tickets, by Eva Crocker | 9 |
| Iteration*, by Annette Conway | 13 |
| Making Bread, by Annette Conway | 17 |
| Walls, by Chad Pelley | 21 |
| Regal Hill, by Josh Pennell | 25 |
| Why is Margaret Crying So Early in the Morning?, by Mary Pike | 29 |
| Raw Turnip, by Dara Squires | 35 |
| Adele, by Deborah Whelan | 39 |
| Moving On, by Kathleen Knowles | 43 |
| City of Villainy, by Christopher Martin | 47 |
| Resistance, by Gerard Collins | 51 |
| The Star of the Sea, by Lisa Porter | 55 |
| A Bone In France, by David C. Kennedy | 59 |
| Merrymeeting, by Danielle Devereaux | 63 |
| Firebug, by Beth Ryan | 67 |
| The Space in Between, by Sharon Bala | 73 |
| Blue Balloons, by Alan W. Davidson | 75 |
| The Victrola, by Michael Finn | 79 |
| Miss Fyfe, by Michael Nolan | 83 |
| The Goat, by Joshua Goudie | 87 |
| Stranger in the Shed, by Samuel Thomas Martin | 91 |
| Written in Bone, by Michael Collins | 97 |
| Burning, by Heidi Mitchell | 101 |
| The Rising, by Chantelle Sears | 105 |
| Caribou, by Laura O'Brien | 113 |
| Salve Regina, by Ellen Alcock | 117 |
| The Visitor, by Michael Collins | 121 |
| Frank Sullivan's Storm, by Val B. Russell | 125 |
| Dinks, by Ed Turpin | 129 |
| Recycling, by Ed Turpin | 133 |
| Undertow, by Keith Collier | 139 |
| Listen to the Wolf, by Owen Whelan | 143 |
| Growing Things, by Vicki Combden Murphy | 149 |

# Our Guys

## By Grant Loveys

*1st-place winner of The Cuffer Prize 2011*

It's getting to the end of the season now and spring's coming on. Our guys are losing a few teeth here and there, spitting them out into empty Tim Hortons cups like wads of old gum they're saving and then leaping back over the bench. I think the boys must feel spring in their teeth first. Kind of like how one day you'd see the buds coming out all at once in Bannerman Park and know something was about to change — maybe their teeth start to loosen up when the weather warms and the ice gets a bit softer. Easier to let them go that way.

Anyway, the other night our guys beat the pads off the other guys' goalie six or seven times, something that, as you know, doesn't happen very often. They won and I won; I put a fair bit of money on it, more than usual, with a new book down in Rabbittown over behind the Sobeys. He said sure that's too much, especially on that crowd, but they're our guys — guys I believe in and always put my money on. And I had a feeling. So when the Lawrence kid got the game winner I got a bit crazy. Vinegar fries flying all over my end of Memorial Stadium and a few people on the other side laughing into their coat sleeves. But six hundred bucks is a big thing when you've got a flattened Black Horse box over the hole in the door.

I always liked that kid, you know? Not that I had any reason to after the way he's been playing, but this time he pulled it off. The thing is, after he poked it in he looked right at me and tapped on his heart. Never met the fella in my life. And he smiled the same way you did. Looked exactly like you for a second. It's hard to take that as just one more weird thing in a world full of them, especially now with you gone. When I see stuff like that, I can picture you pulling strings the rest of us can't even understand and laughing at how stunned we all are to not notice all this strangeness going on in front of our eyes. I remember you telling me about first coming into town and finding all the pavement strange to walk on. Not a strip of asphalt in Spanish Room in the '40s. Well, that's how I feel most of the time these days — unsure, like the ground isn't right under my feet.

I guess the whole thing is all a bit much to believe, really — you fooling around with the game, putting all those pucks in the net just for me. Nobody's got their name written on the world. Every night there's a load of people slopping themselves out of West Side or Dooly's cursing on one team or another and there's probably a few lined up over in Rabbittown with handfuls of cash, too. And I'm sure every one of our guys and the other guys down on the ice were all wishing to whoever that they'd win that one. You couldn't control all that if you wanted to.

When I went down to pick up my winnings, the book looked like he was ready to belt me. Had a few cross words, but I ended up with the money. I thought everything over for a bit on the way back home, and it seems sensible enough that you just walked me into that bet. Maybe gave me that feeling I got about the big money. Nothing fancy, no moving heaven and earth, just a few hundred bucks I can use and a little sign that you're still around somewhere. Seems like something you'd do. You had a few things going, knew your way around, so maybe you just snatched that little favour from wherever He keeps them and got it out the back door without too much commotion.

But who really knows? A fella gets to thinking too much and ends up getting away from himself. And you left me with a lot of time to think. All I know for sure is, just like our guys' poor old wiggly teeth, one day everything goes away and you're just left with holes. You win sometimes and more often you don't, but the time you have with your teeth in your head is what really counts.

Maybe our guys look up in the stands every once in a while and notice you're missing, but then the puck comes along and it's time to think about other things. I'm still up there. The crispy ends on the fries, the way the ice looks so clean right before the period starts — everything seems so much more important now. It's like time got into bed with meaning and every moment ended up pregnant. Does that make any sense? I don't know. I just miss you is all.

*****

GRANT LOVEYS lives in St. John's. His work has appeared in publications locally and throughout North America. In 2010 he won an Arts & Letters award for poetry. He has a new book of poems, Our Gleaming Bones Unrobed, published in September 2012.

# What The Difference Is

### By Chad Pelley

*2nd-place winner of The Cuffer Prize 2011*

The guy sitting next to me tried to pop the top off a Corona with a Bic lighter, and now he's only got half a face. His left cheek is like stretched-thin pink Play-Doh, and there's slots you could fit coins through. Having no eyelashes makes him look like a man-sized baby or almost reptilian, so I'm staring. Cleverly though: side on, so his eyes can't see what my eyes are doing. I Google "What is the purpose of eyelashes," confident he can't see the small screen on my phone, and it turns out this man will be getting a lot of dust in his eyes.

On closer inspection, Bic-man's burnt flesh is a bit like melted plastic that's re-solidified. I know because I had a doll for 12 years, a doll that smelled like my mother did — like limes — that my father threw in the fireplace once to prove a point about "Who sets the rules around here."

He felt so bad the next day that he gave me twenty bucks to buy a new doll, but dolls with nostalgic value that smell like limes are hard to come by. And dead moms can't give you new things to get attached to. Because they are dead. And it's not like I don't know what he and "uncle" Jimmy are up to when they force me out to walk the dog. Sometimes in the rain. Sometimes it's, "Pick up some bread while you're out," too, and I hate that, because sometimes it's not even bread, it's something a 12-year-old girl would't need. So I get that look from the woman at the store, like, "What's a little girl like you doing buying coffee filters on a rainy night, all dripping wet like that?"

I come here to St. Clare's Hospital most nights I'm forced out for a walk. It's like a soap opera minus the commercials. People really do sleep with their best friend's wife, you know, and they do it with a startling regularity. Free health care means a doctor will always be there to stitch up your dumb-busted knuckles. The doctors here know the regulars, by name, and they shake their heads a little slower each time they see them back in again. One time I saw a man's middle finger bone, the bone, because the flesh was torn away. It looked like an eyeball had sprouted on his finger: splayed flesh as eyelids and the white of his bone as the eyeball. He'd punched a wall. Most injuries are the injured person's fault. I've always felt they should segregate the lines into accidents and self-destruction, so the poor seniors who fall over stairs, or whatever, don't have to wait around for the self-destructionists to get stitched back up.

I have a top five too-good-to-be-true-but-true stories from this place:

5.) A kid named Pete lost a chunk of his tongue on a cold bus stop pole on LeMarchant Road. He was testing the myth that isn't a myth at all: tongues stick to cold metal. Of course they do: saying they don't is like saying water doesn't freeze. Because that's what happens: your saliva freezes to the pole. So Pete's dumb. He lost the very tip of it, so his tongue was blunt-edged when he showed me. I Googled what that would mean for Pete, and it was bad news: the front of the tongue is where the "sweet-sensing" tastebuds are. He'd lost the best part of his tongue on a dare, and now his life will be forever bitter. Or salty.

4.) A blonde, university-aged girl was so drunk she kept sliding out of her chair. She liked my boots, she said. And my freckles. And for a few hours I pretended we were best friends. BFFs. Out late getting drunk and stared at by hot guys who wanted something they weren't going to get, because we were class acts, me and my best friend. And then she went home without saying goodbye as I waved to her.

3.) This big — I mean tall and obese — cowboy of a man had a crazy belt buckle. It was a bull with pointy horns. He must have bent over too far and too hard, because he had two puncture wounds in his gut from the horns. Two blood-rimmed holes in his white cotton T-shirt, like two mini bullet holes. But that's not the funny part, this is: he was still wearing the belt buckle, and being very careful about how far he bent forward. Nobody wants another two holes in their gut. He was kind enough to let a crying baby and its mother go ahead of him, but never covered his mouth when he sneezed. I never saw it coming. Little dots all over my T-shirt.

2.) I saw an albino girl in here one day. Gorgeous! And I wanted to touch her for the same reason I want to touch a powdery-looking moth when I see one. Whatever that's all about. She smelled like limes too.

1.) An adorable senior citizen with missing teeth named Harry LeBlanc eating JuJubes in a calculated manner with his four good teeth. He fell off his roof re-shingling. He high-fived me goodbye — and felt cool about it — when they called his name and ruined our chat. I don't know why Harry made Number 1. Numbers 2 through 5 change quite frequently, but Harry's the man. Frozen-tongued Pete was okay too, but didn't have much to say. Pole had his tongue. For a while, whenever it was "time to walk the dog" in the daytime, I'd go to the flower shop on Water Street. There's a cute woman with wavy orange hair who waters those flowers so tenderly, like she wants them to know they're pretty. She's sweet. She always ate strawberry-flavoured candies and shared them. Some days, she'd give me wilting flowers, flowers with "another day left in them," and flash me that white and perfectly square-toothed smile. I'd tell her that her teeth are perfect, but she'd say, "Oh stop it, you" like I'm the only one who's ever said a nice thing to her.

That's the difference between her and me. She can't take a compliment. I intuit she has lousy parents or a mean boyfriend and doesn't defend herself. So I stopped going there. Pitying someone makes them pitiful. It's why I won't let the girl in the corner store see me out buying coffee filters for Dad at midnight. I steal them. I will not be pitiful like that perfectly pretty redhead at the flower shop who I hadn't seen for months, until tonight. Flower Girl is in the emergency waiting room. She's bent over herself, so that her chin is level with her knees and her hair is almost touching the dirty floor. It blows like a curtain every time someone opens the door down the hall.

You're only supposed to leave them on for so long, but she fell asleep with Crest Whitening Strips on her teeth, and now she can't take the pain. I'm Googling her situation for her, how long she'll be in pain and if her teeth are ruined, but her story doesn't make my top five.

*****

*CHAD PELLEY is a multi-award-winning writer from St. John's, and the founder of Salty Ink.com. His first novel,* Away from Everywhere, *won the NLAC's CBC Emerging Artist of the Year award, and was shortlisted for the 2010 ReLit Award and the CAA's Emerging Writer of the Year award.*

# Tickets

**By Eva Crocker**

*3rd-place winner of The Cuffer Prize 2011*

Shayla was taking care of her boyfriend's baby for the day so he could pick up an extra shift. Mike worked at the Weston Bread Factory. He liked it there. He said there was tea and cookies in the break room. They got dental. His sweat smelled of warm wet dough. It was like he was always sweating off a hangover.

The baby's face was a strange version of Mike's. Vicky Lynn had the same wide nostrils but on her face they looked fragile, like something molded out of marzipan. She had his see-through eyelashes. She had his fine red hair but on her it was a mess of tangled curls. The way she was and wasn't him reminded Shayla of a parlor trick. Like wiggling your body through a metal hanger, flipping your eyelids inside out.

Shayla put on a pair of flip-flops by the front door and headed over to the store. Vicky Lynn's baby potbelly was pressed against her side. Cars stopped in both directions to let them cross Queen's Road. It was evening. People were turning on their headlights. Shayla felt the cold on her ankles.

She tapped the top shelf of the Nevada case with her knuckle.

"Five of those." The baby's pale eyelashes dipped down and slowly rose back up again. Vicky Lynn was holding the neck of Shayla's hoodie in both hands. She'd almost been asleep on the couch.

"Five of those." Shayla tapped the second shelf, "And ten of the bottom."

"Five, five, ten?"

"See if you can pick me out some lucky ones."

He tossed one on top of the other till they were a little cardboard mound on the counter.

Vicky Lynn's mother dropped her off that morning. Seeing her, Shayla recognized the ancient alchemy at work in Vicky Lynn's face. The way the baby was both of them and neither of them.

The mother laid the diaper bag and car seat on the sidewalk. She carried her daughter into Shayla's house and Shayla followed with the seat in her arms and the bag digging into her shoulder. They passed the wall of empties in the front porch. Shayla could smell the cat's litter and also the yeast smell Mike brought home with him.

In the kitchen, Vicky Lynn took slow steps toward the cat who was asleep in a square of sun on the linoleum floor.

Shayla was alone with the little girl.

"How about we take a little walk over to the store?" Shayla lifted Vicky Lynn up by the armpits. The baby's eyes weren't dark like Mike's at all, they were her mother's dull blue.

She only spent twenty to begin with and she got fifty back.

Vicky Lynn was sitting on the counter. Shayla would be able to see Mike pull up in front of the house through the front door of the store. She handed the cashier a twenty. She lifted up one of her wad of tickets. She bent the ticket till its back buckled and the little tabs sprang open. Nothing. She bent the second one. Nothing. Vicky Lynn was holding a bag of candy in each hand. She brought her hands together and made the bags smash against each other.

"She's the spit of Mike, she's got his face." The cashier said.

And the third ticket. Fifty dollars. Three gold bells tilted on their sides, signing out.

"Got it."

The cashier turned the key and the cash slid open. Ten, twenty, twenty.

"You're a lucky charm." Shayla rubbed her hand across Vicky Lynn's belly. She picked up the next ticket. Nothing. Nothing. Nothing. Shayla leaned back to see if Mike's car had pulled up.

"Five more of the bottom." She handed him one of her new twenties. It was soft like it'd been through the wash. Nothing. Nothing. Nothing.

Shayla's jeans were tight and she could feel the new twenty and ten scrunched in her pocket. She took the baby back across the road to her little apartment.

Shayla made macaroni and cheese for Vicky Lynn. She melted a hunk of butter and sprinkled grated cheese into it and whipped at it with a fork. She sat Vicky Lynn in her booster seat and snapped the tray into place.

Vicky Lynn dug her hand into the bowl and mashed warm macaroni into her scalp. She ground the white noodles and sauce into her red curls. She looked Shayla right in the eyes while she did it.

The baby fell asleep on the couch. There was still some crusty macaroni close to her scalp. She had fallen asleep with her head in Shayla's lap and her knees drawn up to her belly. Shayla picked the little scabs of melted cheese out of the baby's thin hair. The light of the store's sign projected a yellow glow onto the living room curtains. She eased the Vicky Lynn's head onto the sofa and went to the window and parted the curtain. She could see the cashier hunched over a paper he'd spread out on the lid of the ice cream cooler.

Shayla dragged two chairs in from the kitchen and set them up with their backs to the edge of the couch. There was no way the child could roll off.

The street was empty. Shayla got in line behind some girls whose taxi was idling outside the front door. They were bleached and tanned and made up. They wanted this type of cigarettes and then that type and the key to the beer cooler. The cashier was asking did they have ID. The girls opened their suitcase-sized purses and started taking things out and laying them on the counter. Shayla could see the light on in her living room from where she stood in line.

She spent the last of her new money. She got a big stack of tickets.

"See if you can pick out some lucky ones."

They were so light in her hands. She gave half the pile to the cashier to open. A line of cherries. Shayla ripped the tabs off and laid it on the counter.

"Five bucks."

Mike's car pulled in where the taxi had just pulled out. She saw him see her through the glass in the door. There was no way the baby could roll off. She still had the bottom half of her stack to get through.

*****

*EVA CROCKER lives St. John's and is studying English at Memorial University.*

# Iteration*

*The act of repeating a process with the aim of a desired goal*

## By Annette Conway

*Honourable mention The Cuffer Prize 2011*

When the sun rises in The Narrows, fingers of light paint the houses on Prescott Street red. Although the clapboard is actually green or blue or yellow, the houses all look crimson and she squints in the early light because the reflection off the dew is quite bright and she still has sleep in her eyes.

She copies down in the doorway and her cigarette is soft between her lips and her pink cotton housecoat doesn't reach her knees. She is not wearing underwear and the soft breeze tickles her goose bumps and she feels shivers run up her spine. The smell of last night's rain drifts off the pavement and she knows it will be a cool day because there is no smell of sewage drifting up from the harbour.

There is one more breath in the cigarette and she squeezes it out and into her and lets it go and watches it swirl around her face. She flicks the butt onto the sidewalk and it rolls down the concrete until it stops where the grass grows up between the cracks.

She stretches and her knees crack and her housecoat opens a bit and she pulls it back around her because she doesn't want to give the cab driver coming up the hill something to talk about. She wraps her arms around herself for the heat that is in them and hears the youngsters wake and she goes back inside.

Paul is standing in the kitchen and he chases down his smoke with the instant coffee because they can't afford the real thing. His tool belt is at his feet and he grabs it with purpose when he hears the horn from Bill's truck at exactly 7:20 and he slings it over his shoulder like a purse.

"I'm gone," he says, not yet gone. "You'll be here when I get home?"

"I always am," she says and she always is and there is no malice in her response.

They kiss and she tastes smoke and coffee and their lips against each other's feel like tissue paper dampened by too much time in the basement.

Emily and Jacob are out the door by 8:15 and off to school and the youngest is bundled into the stroller because she has things that must get done. The traffic is lighter on Prescott Street now and the cars have gone to their underground parking and their occupants to their cubicles to pass another day in air that is too old and light that is too dim. She breathes the moist wind and smells the salt and closes her eyes against the sun even thought the sharpness has left it.

Halliday's Meat Market is the last thing on her list and she likes it because it is unlike the large supermarket chains where customers are anonymous nuisances. The butcher is friendly and chatty and he plies his bloody trade with enthusiasm and makes his customers happy and pleased.

"Good morning, Jen," he says and his smile contradicts his blood-smeared apron that looks like a crime scene. "Youngsters packed off to school?" He leans on the counter and his question is sincere and he waits for her to answer.

"Yes, now if I could just get this one gone I'd have her knocked," she says and doesn't mean it because this is her baby and she will miss him and she tucks her hair behind her ears because she knows she is more attractive and it's only Bob after all but she feels she should try.

"Fresh meat?" he says and for a second she forgets where she is and who she is and tries to think of a witty retort that doesn't come.

"It's Wednesday," she says.

"So it is," he says. "The holiday's got me fooled up. I didn't expect you till tomorrow." He searches for the best pieces of beef and he always makes her feel special in his deliberateness and he wraps the meat like a gift in the brown paper and ties the string into a bow.

"Perfect," she says and she means it and she nods at him, approving of the weight of the bundle in her hands.

"Say hello to Paul for me," he says and she says she will and she does.

He comes around the corner to hold open the door and she pushes the stroller out and thanks him as he carries it over the steps. The air feels warmer than it really is and she leaves her jacket undone and walks home like that.

She misses the noonday gun and the sometimes reckless firing of the cannon and the wanton disregard for the confusion caused over the proper time of day. It is time for the baby's nap and she places him in a bassinet while she drinks her tea and scratches pen against paper to harness the words in her head that do not come out nearly as well as they do in her dreams.

It is 3:20 and the bus is never late and it is not late today and it opens its doors for Emily and Jacob and she stands in the brightness of the sun that has moved further west and laughs to see them home safely. They run across the street with papers fluttering in their hands and then grasp the sheets to their chests to stop the colours from flashing in the light.

"What have ye got there?" she says and opens the door so they can get in out of the wind and keep the papers in one piece.

"It's art day today, Mommy," says Emily and passes the painting of yellows and blues to be displayed on the fridge and Jacob, who is smaller, passes his, too.

"My goodness aren't they beautiful," she says and she means it and falls in love with the colours and she takes the prints from last week off the fridge to make way for the new ones. She stands back to have a better look and she tilts her head and squints her eyes and the children smile madly and appreciatively because they are young.

"Won't Daddy love these," she says and it is a statement and not a question because she knows Paul will.

The smell of barley and warmth from the soup meets Paul in the door at 5:20 and the sound of his tool belt on the tiles is loud and sharp. He loves Wednesdays for the soup she makes and the closeness to the weekend when the tenseness leaves his shoulders and the children clamour over them in the morning.

When they are finally tucked in bed and sleeping and the last of the purple sky fades behind the houses, she leans against the step and closes her eyes against the night and she looks like the light is within her. In a few hours the baby will wake at 12:05 as he does and she will nurse him in the quiet of the house and then sleep until she starts over again and she smiles in anticipation.

*****

*ANNETTE CONWAY was born in St. John's. After studying law in Windsor, Ont., she returned to St. John's where she now practices. She lives in Torbay with her partner, their two children and three dogs.*

# Making Bread

### By Annette Conway

*Honourable mention The Cuffer Prize 2011*

Nan cups the flour in her hand, sifts it into the bowl, creating a white cloud in the still air. She adds a little more, shifts the bowl to gauge the amount, adds a little more. The yeast that has been brewing in a bath of warm water in the chipped yellow bowl is added gently and stirred until a fleshy ball of dough emerges. She places the bowl on top of the stove and covers it with a cuptowel. Within an hour the dough pushes the towel upwards as if there is some great swollen beast straining to get outside.

I watch in a combination of fascination and envy as she punches down the mound and then sets to the task of kneading. Her hands, spattered with brown age spots, squeeze and pull the dough, tucking in each end like the sheets at the bottom of a bed as she works it over and over until the feel is to her liking. The tendons in her forearms contract and ripple under her skin. Her brows knit together in concentration until she feels the consistency she desires. She splits the ball into three equal parts and places them side by side in bread pans that are older than me. They are set to rise again. Once ready, she makes the sign of the cross over the top of each pan and then they disappear into the oven.

I look out The Narrows and see a bank of fog hanging off the cliffs blurring the horizon so that I cannot tell where the sky begins and the ocean ends.

*Here he comes, now, here he comes,* Pop says, the smell of barley and hops thick on his words. *The big man about town.* His arms, thick as longers, are crossed on top of his protruding belly, the buttons of his flannel shirt straining, the white of his undershirt peeking out.

Pop doesn't rise to greet Darren. He just flicks another cover off the top of the Black Horse. A swirl of mist curls out of the neck of the bottle. He tips it to his lips.

Nan wipes her hands on the front of her apron leaving handprint dustings like you see at a crime scene. She hugs Darren, her squat body pressed against his like the dough in the tin pans. The edges of her leak out over the side.

*My God, it's some good to see you. You're looking wonderful, just wonderful. Pull up a chair now, I gets you a bite to eat.*

She waddles over to the stove and scrapes some butter into the frying pan. She sets the burner on high. Nan lifts the fresh cod she sent me to buy this morning from Taylor's out of a bowl. She lays the fillets on some paper towels and pats them dry, the silver white skin glistens. She hums as she dips the fillets in flour, then egg, then flour again with a sprinkle of salt and pepper on top. She sets them into the pan and a spray of melted butter showers the stovetop.

Darren gives me a clout on the shoulder. I grin up at him.

*How's it going, my buddy.*

My cousin Darren freshly home from Fort McMurray. Four years working on heavy equipment, fours years away from this island.

*You should see the size of the wheels on the trucks I'm driving Seamus. Bigger than this house, b'y.*

I watch a trawler cut through the maggoty brown waters of the harbour, the ripples cutting out behind it reminds me of the first time I went trouting. I rode across the barrens on Pop's shoulders, ten years ago, when I was just a small boy and Pop a strong man. Me, Pop and Darren going trouting at Pop's secret spot. Darren threaded the worm on the hook for me and cast it in the pond. The bobber struck the water and circles floated towards the shore. I got a bite on the first cast and reeled it in as they cheered. The trout flipped and shuddered as I flicked it onto the ground. Its gills flared furiously searching for air and I watched it struggle. Pop's giant hand closed around it, gripping tightly as it thrashed and wiggled, and then he smashed its head against a rock until it lay still. I couldn't tear my eyes from the gelatinous slime that coated the stone, the sudden stillness of that fish.

*It's suffering like that, my son. You can't just leave it there*, he said gently. He cast my line out again and tossed the fish in our bucket.

The cod sizzles on the pan as Nan flips it over, another spatter of butter sprays upward. Pop's beer is finished and he is looking out the kitchen window, his fingers tapping lightly on the formica table. His eyes are pink-rimmed and watery and there is a slight shudder to his left hand. He sighs deeply, the breath squeezing out of his lips like a dropped accordion, but he says nothing.

*This is delicious, Nan, Darren says,* stuffing a piece of fish in his mouth. *B'y, you just can't beat fresh fish.*

*Don't suppose you got anything like that up along, did ye?* Pop finally speaks. *Bet all your big Alberta money couldn't buy fish like ye gets at home, could it?*

Darren says nothing as he eats the cod. His eyes are half closed and dreamy as if he'd been drinking too much.

*I got a nice piece of land down in Torbay, Pop,* Darren says. *Me and Angela are going to build a spot down by the ocean.*

There is no answer from Pop, he's looking out at the harbour from his perch at the kitchen window. The lines around his eyes have drawn them tight, as if he is squinting against the sun, though it's foggy outside.

*Hey Pop, didn't you hear? Darren's moving around the bay,* I say taking a bite of the cod Nan has set before me.

*I suppose you won't be fit to look at now with your big Mac money,* he says and snorts at his own joke. His tone carries a note of despair borne of regret and guilt. *Gonna build a big old house I suppose.* His breath is hard and sharp.

The smell of the bread seeps out of the oven. I can picture the butter melting over the top of it. I can taste it warm and sticky in my mouth.

*Yes, Pop. We made enough money so we hardly needs a mortgage.* Darren scrapes his plate clean and leans back in the chair.

Pop wheezes and reaches down by the side of the table and picks up the plastic mask attached to the small canister beside him. Nan helps secure the elastic around the back of his head. His breath punctuates the silence until the hiss of the machine takes over.

Pop looks back out the window. *I wouldn't mind a bit of that bread,* he says to no one in particular, the words muffled inside the plastic, his nostrils flaring and straining against the world.

# Walls

## By Chad Pelley

*Honourable mention The Cuffer Prize 2011*

It's a frozen tear under his eye, or it's another snowflake. They're thick tonight, the snowflakes. They're shattered clouds, and he wants to be buried in them. He's sick of walking, and fighting his way through the sharp knives of wind. He's walking along the edge of the highway, somewhere between Terra Nova and Clarenville, and he only knows that much because he passed that orange North Atlantic Gas station. The lights were off. The power's gone. Everywhere. His car got stuck in the unploughed snow about ten minutes after he passed the station, and punching the steering wheel didn't get him unstuck. So he dug beneath his tires with ungloved hands, like a dog digging up earth.

He's breathing out ghosts, puffs of white air, and the snow is cold quicksand. He has to yank his legs back out after each step, and his ankles are cut sore from cold snow. His socks are soaked and squeezing out puddles with each step. Gusts of wind are walking through him like frigid phantoms, one after another. They're getting inside him, and melting. He imagines his blood flow freezing like a river. Red ropes beneath his skin. Cold feels like heat after long enough. Or it feels like a pressed bruise, and his hands are numb and throbbing like they've been hit by hammers. You don't think about putting on gloves when your son is missing. You leave the front door wide open with the snow blowing in. You bang your head off the outside of the car as you're jumping into it.

He came home and the babysitter's car wasn't there and his son was gone. Nate. Not even three. He put two hands on either side of the porch doorframe and yelled hello, knowing no one was going to answer him. It was just to fill the moment with action. To break it. To shatter the moment when the panic started. He walked to the kitchen table hoping for a note, an explanation. *I took the little man out for ice cream.* But no one leaves the house in a storm like that. His legs turned to sand and he sat down. Maybe there was an accident. She'd cut a finger, deeply, dicing vegetables, or Nate stuck a hand in the fireplace again. But she would have called his cell. He checked under the table like maybe the note had fallen.

He walked to Nate's room taking breaths so deep his stomach popped like balloons each time. Half of Nate's toys and clothes were gone. Stray T-shirts like coloured puddles on the floor.

Then the dash to the door. A left boot on a right foot and he almost didn't notice. Terror like a ton of fire in his chest. And now this slow pacing along the highway towards nothing. She'd said she was from Clarenville, the babysitter, so he was hoping she'd gotten stuck in the snow too. He pictured Nate twisted and crying and pressing a hand against the back windshield, screaming out to him. If he found her, Clara, it would be the first time he ever hit a woman. There would be blood in the snow and he'd leave her there.

He'd hired the babysitter off a sheet of paper on a bulletin board in a convenience store. The press will have a field day, and ten thousand mothers will shake their heads. He won't blame them. It was an irresponsible oversight, a desperate move, and it never would have happened if his wife wasn't calling another house home now. He was already shifting blame, as he blew heat into cupped hands. This needing a babysitter; that was something Karen had always dealt with.

He'd met his wife the same way he met every woman: like a truck into a wall. He had a way of romanticizing the idea of a woman, and falling immediately in love with that fabrication. The way a woman picked through the apples in the grocery store. That was enough to assume things about her.

Karen was a Chemistry professor at MUN, teaching ionic bonds and rates of reaction across the hall from where he taught genetics. One day during a midterm, his class no louder than the sound of 20 pencils scratching out best guesses, he'd watched her talking about chemistry. She had fake plastic atoms in her hand, demonstrating how the smallest change changes everything, and her voice had a way of snagging on C-K formations. Words like baCK sounded irrationally erotic in her mouth. From that day on, he'd let his class go a few minutes early, to sit in a silent room and soak up her cloud-soft voice. He'd fall off all her words like a cliff.

She'd confronted him over it one day. They'd both left their classrooms at the same time, and that awkward walk down the quiet hall needed space filled. "You're making me look bad," she said. "I keep my students the full class but you let yours out early all the time." But she'd said it with a smile, tucking hair gently behind her ear. She had a grace that softened his bones. She'd made a shark of his eyes. Ravenous.

Six years later she left him saying, "Your problem is you could never love a woman as much as you loved your assumptions about that woman." He'd argued she was wrong, because he was certain that she, Karen Hill, was perfectly irreplaceable. That post-it note grip between their lips when they kissed, and the perfect weight of her arm on his chest when they slept at night. He swore it was irreplaceable, yet she was gone and he was still alive. Her purple bathrobe still hung on the back of his bedroom door like six years of love crying out for a second chance, but it was just a piece of cloth, faded to white at the elbows, and rendered bumpy by the passing of time.

One hundred steps into that endless snow, stomping towards nowhere, changed everything. The frozen tears on his face, digging under his tires with his bare hands, the overwhelming hollow feeling of helplessness. He could live without Karen. If he had to. It was a violent exorcism, letting her go. Like fighting off a cancer. Sweaty sleepless nights with memories poking and prodding him, and thoughts of Karen embedded in bone, dominating daydreams, and hidden deep in intangible places where even time couldn't reach its claws.

It's colder now. The wind like slaps and punches. He can't feel his hands, not even when he bites them. A snowflake in the eye is like a finger when it hits you at the right angle. He's hauling his legs out of that white quicksand; every step twice as hard as the last. But he'd walk forever, towards nothing, just to feel like he was one step closer to Nate. He'd die before he let that child out of his life. And realizing Karen was right, that she was replaceable — in a way that Nate wasn't — was as haunting as the thought of death.

# Regal Hill

## By Josh Pennell

*Honourable mention The Cuffer Prize 2011*

On the street where I grew up, the higher up on the hill your house, the tougher your family. Our house was at the very top and my three brothers wore that reputation on their knuckles. They could each smack the lips off a horse. I, on the other hand, lived in the long shadow they cast down over Regal Hill. I lived in the house at the very top and I lost every fight I ever fought.

Now as much as my brothers took care of me, if I decided to raise my fists they had enough respect for the hill to stay out of it. So by the age of 13 I had more stitches in me than one of Nan's quilts. And whenever they fell out or the doctor pulled them from me, I put them in an envelope on the windowsill in my room along with a few rattled teeth. That unraveled blue ribbon allowed me to stroll the hill with my head held half mast. Walking into a fight you might win takes no guts at all, in my opinion. Try walking into one knowing you'll lose.

Ronald Drover lived in the house at the very bottom of the hill. His father drove a semi and always took the scenic route home. His finely crafted mother worked the pool hall at the bottom of the street called The Brass Rack. "There's a golden rack at the Brass Rack," was the word all over the hill. Needless to say, Ronald could scrap. He was at the bottom of the hill trying to fight his way up and I was at the top trying to do the same.

The only damage I caused the last time I fought him was my knuckles grazed the scruff under his chin and came away rashy. One of the Catholic Cloths spotted him pummeling me and that was that. I guess One Regal Hill wasn't the spot for a fella only too willing to try and move his family up to higher ground by beating others into it. A week later the house was empty and that was the last we saw of the golden rack. The only wound that never healed.

We all watched with curiosity knowing full well the lousy tattoo that came with the mortgage of One Regal Hill. Then one day in spring a rusted blue time capsule pulled up with a rawboned mother, her hair tied in pigtails in a cheerless effort to look younger.

Her brother moved her in. When he rumbled away, a young fella was standing in front of the truck, a cap tight over his eyes and a jean jacket swinging from his limbs. His head was so low he looked intimidated by the new leaves sprouting above him. We thought him too young first but then he showed up in my grade. Old enough to bleed. Old enough to butcher.

But if ever there was a young fella who belonged at the very bottom of Regal Hill it was Jimmy Spence. He hardly lifted his head, manoeuvring around poles and mailboxes with a sixth sense. On the hill there had to be an opening, some wound to slip your salty fingers into. Somebody who lived at the bottom with no will to move up couldn't be beaten down any further. I should have left it at that but the envelope on my windowsill was ready to burst. Jimmy looked like he had nothing to lose but I just felt like I had never won anything.

Louie O'Rourke was giving out smokes for a smack on the arm. Our shoulders turned black as our lungs. I had half a deck on me but wanted two from Louie for reasons of prominence. I was rubbing my shoulder with tears in my eyes when I saw Jimmy following his shoes.

"Hey Jimmy, wanna smoke?"

He made eye contact and it was like he couldn't find the spot on the ground where he left off. I saw the wound.

"Have a smoke!" I called out again and slid one my shoulder bought down from my ear.

Everybody watched Jimmy shuffle over with his fingers held out. As soon as he touched the butt I clocked him on the arm and down he went.

"They're a bruise each," I said and pulled down my shirt to show the currency.

A swell of laughter through the crowd. I couldn't stop now. I stood over him and held out the other smoke as though he could pull himself up with it. It was too much for even Jimmy Spence to walk away from. He stood and I lay into his other shoulder. His legs triangled, his hands sliding on the ground as he bent from the waist. More nervous laughter and I smiled to egg it on.

Whether Jimmy grabbed a hold of me to pull me down or reached to keep himself up I'll never know, but down we both went and the laughter really went up this time. Wiping the muddy snow from my neck and face, I caught Jimmy out of the corner of my eye. His eyes met mine and I guess Jimmy Spence tossed a little salt my way then.

When the first smack actually connected I almost fell back in surprise but managed to lay into his face again before I went over top of him. Then it was right after right after right with my left holding Jimmy's bunched up skin and collar. I was breathing so hard I was drooling.

One of my brothers tossed me aside and I got up to go back at him. Jimmy stared up at me with his eyes bulging and his face bleeding from so many places he looked like a partridgeberry tart. I loomed over him in a fit of the shakes. He pulled himself back across the ground and took off down the hill. The crowd stared until I walked away with my head down, my feet filling in Jimmy's footprints until I made the turn to my house.

I never bothered to go to the doctor, though my hands could have used a stitch or two.

When I did come out of my room my brothers wouldn't speak to me. I got similar treatment from the crowd in the neighbourhood. At least for a spell. That didn't last long, though. Soon all was in order again. Except for one thing. Jimmy never showed up to class. I went by his house with a rare Regal Hill apology but nobody answered. Then one day, there was the blue time capsule all filled up again. I saw Jimmy's lowered head through the window as they drove away.

That night I sat in my window and held the envelope in my hands.

I thought about all the wounds those stitches tried to hold closed. I opened the window and poured the envelope out, the teeth clinking as they struck the drain pipe on the way down to the sidewalk, the stitches sailing out onto the night wind that was blowing from the very top to the very bottom of Regal Hill.

*****

*JOSH PENNELL is a journalist living in St. John's, Newfoundland and Labrador. He won The Cuffer Prize in its inaugural year and has also placed third in the contest.*

# Why is Margaret Crying So Early in the Morning?

## By Mary Pike

*Honourable mention The Cuffer Prize 2011*

Margaret's sharp burst of anguish fills the Home's dayroom like a summer's thunderstorm — sudden and short.

Unlike a cleansing thunderstorm, it fails to freshen the urine-tinged air.

I look up from kissing my grandmother hello. Margaret is positioned in the middle of the room. She leans forward and sideways over the armrest of the high-backed chair into which she is strapped. Wordless, she stares at us with tortured intensity before lowering her eyes to arthritic entwined fingers. I guess Margaret to be late forties. Brown hair tucked behind her ears, bright coral lipstick complementing her sweater, a pant cuff hitched up behind her knee, caught during a struggle to cross her legs.

The Home's dining room doubles as its dayroom. Eight square tables ring an open space. A small kitchenette forms one wall and a 20-inch television is parked high on an opposite shelf. Female residents sit at the tables or slump in wheelchairs scattered around the room. Most stare at the floor.

Among the residents move three aides, or licenced practical nurses, or nurses. I'm never sure who is who as all sport two-piece pajama-like outfits and no nametags. I'll call them caregivers, because in a Home this is how I see their role. They glance toward, then ignore Margaret, and continue their morning ministrations. They position chairs in front of the mute television. They fiddle with the radio volume; VOCM plays its toe-tapping Saturday morning Irish-Newfoundland music. Women are wheeled in and out for toileting and bathing.

"Don't take off me clothes," a lady calls to the air as a caregiver propels her through the room. "I'm going home now."

Nan takes my hand in both of hers and rubs her cheek against my palm. She closes her eyes and purrs soft sounds of contentment.

A guttural moan catches in Margaret's throat.

"How are you?" I say to Nan's tablemate, the lady with the bearing of a queen. A French knot crowns her thick white hair. With her cultured pearl necklace and double strand of wrist pearls, I can imagine her captivating fellow waltzers at a long-ago ball.

"Your pearls are beautiful," I say.

She raps her jeweled wrist on the table. "I don't want to be here."

This voice and noise rouses her neighbours. A septuagenarian uncoils from her slumped position and flicks her tongue in and out, in and out, as if testing the atmosphere. Another grins like she harbours a wonderful secret. She dry washes her hands over and over again.

"Is this okay for me," laughs a jolly grandmother, brandishing a piece of toast. Her rolls of belly fat shake.

"Is this okay for me?" She tap-dances the toast on the table and sings to the radio: "Yes indeed" tap "I do" tap "love you" tap. She brings the toast to her eyes for close examination before tonguing its brown crust. "It's yucky." She tosses it on the table.

I turn to a voice muttering, "I feel like doing this." In a blink the woman whips her green sweater up over her cotton bra.

I walk over and touch her arm. "You shouldn't do that," I say.

"Why not?" She giggles.

A male caregiver shuffles close.

"What do you have there?" she says, grabbing his crotch. He performs a quick side step and lays his sloshing Tim Hortons coffee on a table.

"Pull down your sweater, duckie," he says. He takes the centre of the ribbed waistband between thumb and forefinger and tugs until the sweater again covers her.

"I thought only men acted like that," I say. He half-smiles and doesn't make eye contact.

He moves to a woman with multi-coloured eyewear. But no, the purple bridge of her nose connects blue and red bruises that circle her eyes. He lowers his face to hers.

"Where are your glasses?" he says.

She peers in near-sighted confusion. "Somewhere in my room."

"Do you have your teeth in?"

"My top ones."

"Where're your bottom teeth?"

"Somebody stole 'em."

"Can I go home with ye?" calls a plaintive voice from a corner of the room.

"Yes," says the caregiver, not looking at the resident.

"Can I go home with ye?" she calls again.

"Just look at her poor legs," says Nan. I see a pair of bird thin legs encased in tights. Their equally thin owner paddles her legs in synchronized futility against the floor; her locked wheelchair doesn't move.

I need breathing space.

To Nan I say, "I'll be back in a minute. I'll get you some chocolate from your room."

"Good morning," I say to Margaret as I walk past.

"Errrr," she says and lurches forward as though to follow me.

A resident plucks at my sleeve. She murmurs in hope. "Please, stop for awhile and tell I about yourself?"

"Can I give some of the ladies chocolate?" I ask at the nurse's station.

"Not right now. I'm just filling in and I've no idea who's diabetic and who's not."

It's 11 a.m. but the station's wall clock shows 4:35. The minute hand jerks forward a second, then jerks back. Jerks forward. Jerks back.

A caregiver walks past holding a large clear plastic bag full of shitty Depends.

I lay three chocolates on the table in front of Nan. She arranges and rearranges them like she's playing a shell game. Guess which one hides the maraschino cherry? Her finger hovers over each before she chooses one and pops it in her mouth. "Mmmmm," she says. "Mmmmm."

"My mother is having trouble hearing," I overhear a visitor.

The caregiver peers into the woman's ears. "She doesn't have her hearing aid in."

"She doesn't wear one."

"Yes she does."

"She's never worn one in her life."

"Oh, it must have been the woman in the bed before her."

Nan wraps the remaining chocolates in a tissue. "I'll be saving these for Mommy. She likes a little something before she goes to bed."

She fumbles with the waistband of her slacks and tucks the chocolates between the band and her blouse.

"I'm hungry," moans a woman.

"You just finished breakfast," says a caregiver.

"Did I?"

"Poor thing," says Nan. "She doesn't know she ate."

A diminutive elder positions her varicosed hands on the edge of her table. She presses to move her wheelchair backwards. Instead, the table inches closer to a younger woman on the opposite side. The younger pushes back with a grunt and a screech of table leg on tile.

"Stop it," calls a resident. "She's an old lady."

"Ah, shut up," drools the pusher. She shoves harder and soaks her knee from the exertion.

"Can I go home with ye?" calls the voice from the corner.

"You're not going home," yells the green-sweatered woman. With the rhythm of a lit beacon she flashes her bra.

This time, Margaret's burst of anguish rises and rises and swirls around the room like a tornado. The wretched howls peak to one long drawn out note before dropping to a wail that leaves her and the Home breathless.

"Tut, tut," says a caregiver into the silence. "Why is Margaret crying so early in the morning?"

*****

*MARY PIKE is a fiction and non-fiction writer who has received awards in the Newfoundland and Labrador Arts & Letters Competition and a mentorship with WANL's Emerging Writers Mentorship Program. She has stories published in* Telling Truth, A Collection of Essays, *the* The Cuffer Anthology Volume II *and* Paragon IV.

# Raw Turnip

## By Dara Squires

*Honourable mention The Cuffer Prize 2011*

We didn't play cops and robbers like the kids up in the Catholic subdivision. With their sprinklers and their play-sets, they thought they were better than us. The only thing they were good for was a brief friendship around Halloween; an invite to go trick-or-treating up there meant less walking and more loot.

They had hopscotch boards permanently painted onto their driveways, and store-bought swing-sets cemented in their backyards. We had half-rotten tire-swings and The Farmer.

The Farmer didn't have a name. He was just the cranky old man who owned a farm next to my house.

Our favourite game was piss-off-The-Farmer. He'd run around like a dog chasing its tail trying to keep us off his land. Daniel and Joe would walk, brazen as blue-arse flies, down the centre of the hayfield while Laurie and I would scamper through the tall grass and run — double-bent — for the river. Eventually he'd notice the boys and haul out his BB gun. They were always brave enough to take a bullet for us.

Meanwhile, Laurie and I would be stripped down to our underwear, hauling up buckets of water. The boys would catch up and together we'd throw water at the cows. Some of them just stood there. You could even throw it right in their face, and all they'd do is blink. But we had bets on which ones would go wild. The Farmer would come running to see what had made the cows so anxious but by the time he got there we'd have ducked under the culvert and run along the river out to the turnip fields by the road.

After we horsed around for a while in the water, we'd go pull turnips.

Usually we'd eat just a few bites and throw them back in the field.

But one time I snuck a knife down the pocket of my pants so we could cut right into the core of them and eat the sweet, raw centre. Daniel, being the oldest, had the honour of cutting.

He jabbed the blade into the dirt-clung globe — used the tip of it to trace its quarters, one for each of us. But as he cut deeper the blade jumped away and gashed his hand. I grabbed his hand and looked at him, through hanks of wet hair, as I sucked on the wound to get the blood to stop.

I still remember the tang; his skin tasted different, saltier and sweatier. And his blood was thick — like eating soil almost.

I thought they were Jewish because they never went to church. But it turns out Daniel and Laurie were atheists. Their parents tried to explain it to me that night over barbecued hotdogs and stolen potatoes. But I didn't quite get it. Jews were exotic and mysterious; his parents were just dippy and complained a lot about the prime minister and the schools.

After supper the three of us played around in the yard for a while; a lazy game of spotlight and a more exciting game of Dare. Laurie dared me to pee in The Farmer's field the next time we cut through and I had to swear I would.

Later, Daniel and I zigzagged through the hay so he could walk me home. He said he'd jump in front of any bullet, even though I told him my brothers had shot me plenty of times with their BB guns. He wrapped his arm around me, even though I wasn't cold. But I let him think I was.

It was too dark for The Farmer to see us anyway. So dark that I tripped on a furrow and went straight onto my knees. I started to cry, not, like Daniel thought, because I was hurt. I had taken my mother's favourite broomstick skirt from her closet to wear that night, pulling it up under my arms and belting it around my waist. It was the closest I could come with my cutoff shorts and Strawberry Shortcake T-shirts to anything appropriately ethnic for supper with Jews.

My mother, of course, didn't know I had taken it. And now I'd gotten it muddy and maybe ripped. And they weren't even Jews anyway. And even though I hardly had enough chest to hold up a strapless dress, I had enough that Daniel should've noticed. But the only one who did was their creepy cousin who had dropped by with a two-four and some moose after supper.

And now Daniel had seen me crying, which was even worse than everything else; the atheists, torn skirt and creepy cousin combined.

But when I looked up at him, it was like he hadn't noticed at all. He was staring at me with a look on his face like the one he got right before he and Joe had run through the bull's field: like he was at once utterly present and far away.

"Your ...umm..."

He didn't have to say — I felt the coolness on my chest. The skirt had slipped down.

"Oh," I whispered, wanting to lean into him and make him touch me. All evening I'd been trying to get his attention. Only problem was now that I had it, it was too strong — he couldn't move.

"Ouch. Shit!" he shouted as his cheek collapsed inwards in a wave. A speck of blood flecked to the surface of his skin. His eyes met my confusion. Then I knew. The Farmer had got him.

"Fuck you! You could've taken out his eye!" I screamed into the night air.

All we heard in response was a grunt.

Daniel looked at me, hand on his face, dripping blood. His eyes still had that faraway look, like getting shot had sent him permanently somewhere else.

I couldn't see him, but the stench of old cigarettes and stale cow piss rolled off The Farmer like the steam from the ditches on a hot day. He was close. Close enough I could hear his old man breathing — hoarse and hacky.

"Fuck you and your stupid cows!" I shouted at him as I struggled up, throwing clods of dirt into the darkness.

One of the fistfuls thudded more hollow-sounding than the others. We heard him gasp a ratchety, snotty breath. Then silence.

"Do you think he's dead?" Daniel asked, finally coming to.

I didn't know. But I was cold and muddy and blood was dripping down his arm. I figured The Farmer got what was coming to him, same as us. "Just winded," I whispered as I snagged the skirt upwards, looking down to adjust it.

When I looked up, he was gone. A cow's startled lowing, followed by a couple quick splashes, signaled his receding path. I stood alone, satched and shivering in the dark field — then picked my way home, over the barbed wire fence and on to bed.

I had no use for The Farmer's field after that — never met Laurie's dare.

The next week Daniel's family moved to the Catholic subdivision where the schools were better. They never invited me for Halloween.

*****

*DARA SQUIRES grew up in the Goulds and became a townie through amalgamation. Her three children, two puppies, and freelance writing career keep her busy. She writes after midnight.*

# Adele

### By Deborah Whelan

*Honourable mention for The Cuffer Prize 2012*

It was late spring when Adele March came to stay at her uncle's house in Tea Cove. Ramona had never seen hair like Adele's. It was as red as hot coals in the grate. Mom said she left her husband in Oklahoma and came back to Newfoundland and that's what happens when you marry a Yank, as if that meant Adele was to be pitied. Mom had her over for fresh pan-fried halibut the very day she moved in.

And of course, cards, too — Adele had to come over for cards. Mom said she shouldn't be by herself so much. So the next Saturday evening, Adele, Uncle Fred and Aunt Josie were over to play 120s. Ramona sat in her usual spot on the settee beside the stove with her nose buried in a book. Sometimes she would let the book drop as if she'd fallen asleep while she listened to the gossip that floated around her ears. She was the Amazing Disappearing Ramona, not noticed but hearing all.

After losing three games in a row, the men gave up on cards and took their drinks out on the verandah. That was when Adele started in about "Buzz who stung worse than a bee" as the women huddled around the table like witches.

Adele fished a cigarette from her pack of Pall Malls. Her nails were sharp pink hooks. "Buzz wouldn't allow me to have my own friends, and I couldn't go anywhere without him. I couldn't wear lipstick or even coloured panties." Her eyes bugged out of her face as she leaned forward. They were smeared with makeup the colour of wet seaweed. "He beat me once just because he could see my brassiere through my blouse."

Mom blushed. Aunt Josie sniffed.

"Those Yanks are all the same," Adele hissed through clenched teeth. "My dear, I could tell you stories that would curl your hair."

Aunt Josie fluffed her perm. Mom glanced over at Ramona and cleared her throat. "I think I'll put the kettle on now, and I made some nice molasses buns." As Aunt Josie swooped up the cards to clear the table, Ramona followed Adele as she stepped outside on the verandah and sat next to Dad on the bottom step. Uncle Fred studied the sky from the rocking chair and spat into the spittoon between his legs. The night was warm for May. A moon like a yellow balloon painted the cloud edges white.

"I hear you make the best homebrew on the shore." Adele's voice tinkled as she leaned toward Dad and took the glass of homebrew from his hand. She sipped, then drank some more. She didn't seem to notice Ramona leaning over the railing. Mom always said she was a ghost slinking around with her books while everybody else came bounding down the stairs like bulls.

Ramona wasn't sure how she felt about Adele. That took some thinking. It was like when she started a new book. Sometimes the cover, the title and the exciting bits printed on the back didn't even come close to the truth, and the story would take her breath away. She would read slowly, tasting every page. But there was junk, too, no matter how pretty the book was — not that she ever failed to finish a book once she started. But the dream wasn't real and she wasn't sad to leave that world. People were like that, especially adults. Kids usually didn't have covers, just pages.

Adele spoke quietly. Ramona couldn't hear over the clattering of plates and the whistling of the kettle from the kitchen. Dad laughed and Ramona edged closer, intent on hearing any stories that she might miss, especially one that could make her father happy.

"Tea's ready!" Mom called out. Dad jumped and Adele moved away from him. Homebrew spilled over the step. Ramona flinched, expecting cross words from her father. "There's more where that came from," he said as he patted Adele's shoulder through her silky green blouse. Adele smiled up at him and Ramona decided she really didn't like her at all.

It was an evening like that one, just after school finished for the summer and three days before Ramona's eleventh birthday, that Mom called to her from the verandah as she threw a ball for Skippy.

The sun had just dipped into the ocean, the only sound a late fisherman putt-putting into his wharf. She expected the usual: come in and get ready for bed. Instead Mom said, "Why don't we go for a walk up the shore? It's a nice evening for it."

A walk up the shore and it was almost dark! "Come on, Skippy!" Ramona started across the field.

"Put Skippy in the porch. You know how he barks at his own shadow."

She wanted to ask, who is gonna mind? But Mom sounded like she was already miles away. Ramona held her tongue and called Skippy inside.

"We'll walk as far as Scevior's and stretch our legs," Mom said.

"Maybe we'll meet Dad along the way," Ramona said. He had left the house, whistling, after supper. "I saw him walk up along the beach."

Mom nodded and took her hand, still sticky from Skippy's drool. The world turned navy blue as they walked up the hill, the only light coming from the stars and the lamp-lit windows that stained the grass in stretched rectangles. It was like walking up to heaven with all the stars twinkling and welcoming her. Down the shore, the ocean breathed in and out.

Before they rounded the turn to Scevior's, Mom stopped at the green gate to March's house. "I wonder if your father's there. Adele said her stove was smoking bad. He was going to see to the chimney." Mom kept clearing her throat like there was a bone stuck in it. She pulled her sweater tight around her shoulders. "Since we're here, we may as well just peek in the window and see if he dropped by."

Ramona followed her through the gate and up the path and stood on tiptoe to see over the window ledge. And there he was: sitting at the table beside Adele, drinking wine and laughing like she had never ever seen her stern father laugh before. Adele wore a shiny dress that was almost the colour of her hair.

"He's there! Let's go in!"

"Shhh, Ramona! No. We'll just go on home. We won't disturb him when he's working."

"But he's not working. He must be finished. He could walk home with us."

"No. It's time for bed anyway." Mom's voice was a shivery whisper, like when she'd told Ramona her Nan had gone to heaven. Her eyes were bright as she leaned close. "And our little walk is just between us. I know you're good at keeping secrets. Promise?"

She promised. Suddenly, she wanted to hug her mother hard, to bury her face in that old scratchy sweater so she could lose the sick feeling in her stomach. Instead, she took her hand.

They walked home, the silence broken by June bugs pock-pocking their brown bodies against fences. The stars were dimmer now, like they were swimming underwater.

*****

*DEBORAH WHELAN lives in Hearts Delight-Islington. She is a member of WANL, an avid short-story writer and has been short-listed for The Cuffer Prize three times.*

# Moving On

## By Kathleen Knowles

She shouldn't have come. It was over between her and Bernie years ago. But here he was, dead. She was nearly conquered by the smells — flowers, perfume and some chemical that Amanda didn't dare even think about. At least today she knew that Bernie was where he was supposed to be. The small chapel was only half full, everybody bolt upright, like statues carved into the pews, threatened, perhaps, by the sporadic bursts from the organ.

There was his crowd up front: Bill and crazy Bruce and poor stunned Mrs. Somers sobbing to beat the band. The old man, crooked bastard, probably drunk, squished into a suit, staring at the floor. Deaf as Aunt Sheila's cow when he wanted to be. The latest wife, Melissa, Michelle, whatever.

Bernie, you frigger. Things could have been so fine for us. You sure could talk a girl around when you were on the beer — how you loved a small woman, loved dark hair. What you really loved was anybody'd come across.

The minister slid in through a side door bearing the cadaverous look of a mainlander who's just survived his first Newfoundland spring. He glided forward without seeming to move his feet, opened a folder, and cleared his throat.

"My dear friends. We are gathered, on this saddest of occasions, to celebrate the life, and honour the memory, of a man whose tragic death has shocked us deeply. The sudden departure of a fine young man, such as…" he consulted his papers, "James Aloysius Newton, is a bitter blow, but we must rest our faith in God's greater plan, which is often difficult for mere mortals to comprehend."

Amanda started. Who the hell is James Newton?

"My deepest condolences to James' parents Rowena and Alphonse, and to his widow Florence and their darling daughters…" he peered at his papers, "Jessica and Sharon. Out of your weakness shall come strength. Out of your tears shall come joy. Out of your loneliness shall come hope."

I'll be damned. He's reading the wrong speech. Well, Bernie's dead. I guess a funeral's a funeral. No such thing for my little angel. Bernie never even knew about him, a boy, I just know it. Couldn't wait to tell him the news, then on my way home from Dr. Grandy's there's him and that streel from the bar going into the Guvnor's hotel. "Just a bit of fun is all," he said, "Don't be gettin' on about it." I never did get to tell him, lost it before he knew a thing.

The minister stared heavenwards: "Tragedy strikes swiftly and unexpectedly; but," he sounded disappointed, "life goes on."

Bernard had called himself a self-made man. "Not like those bloody MUN types with flag poles up their arses." He and his buddy Jake ran a business together, odd jobs when the spirit moved them. But they had bad luck with customers. "You wouldn't believe how they keep barking at us to come back and finish stuff or change something." Summertime, they'd dart down to Fortune, meet up with friends from St. Pierre, drive around to campsites selling booze from the back of the pickup. "No stamps into it, but there's bucks to be had all the same."

Maybe she shouldn't have made such a fuss. Mum told her it's just as well to ignore it, pretend she hadn't seen him. He would have settled down when he found out about the baby, wouldn't he? She never told a soul, but everybody except Bernie seemed to know the details of her emergency trip to the clinic.

Story was that Bernie died from a fall off a roof he was repairing. No way in hell that was true. He'd always said there was no such thing as a roof that didn't leak in Newfoundland, so why bother? Her friend Krista told her not to breathe a word, but she'd heard the real story from her cousin, twice removed, who was dating Jake's uncle's buddy. Bernie had been having it on with Brendan Coppin's wife, and one night when Bren arrived home early Bernie panicked and jumped out the window.

"You should hear Jake tell it," Krista had laughed. "Just like in the stories. He tore ligaments in his ankle and broke his wrist. But the best of it was that he landed in a whack of stinging nettles and had to stay put until the coast was clear. He was covered all over, and I mean all over, in a savage rash. And then it was after getting infected. It's the penicillin shot killed him. Never even knew he was allergic."

The minister struggled on. "James was a family man."

Right, thought Amanda. He loved families so much he had a few of them.

"Teacher, Scout leader, volunteer at the animal shelter, James was a man you could rely on."

I guess his poker buddies would agree. He never missed a night in our four years.

Bernard's mother was crying more quietly now, beaming through her tears. She had known all along that her son was a saint.

I guess no one's going to tell buddy that he's got the wrong corpse. Wouldn't Bernie be getting a hoot out of this?

A collective intake of breath when the Reverend asked: "I wonder if any of James' friends or family would be comforted by saying a few words."

Slowly, Bernard's father got to his feet, steadied himself against the pew in front of him. "Well my son, sir; myself and my wife are right moved by all the kind things you said about our dear boy. There's nar word could be added to such a beautiful speech."

People stood to leave, chatting and sharing their fears of the better weather of late. The closed casket remained in place. Amanda approached it tentatively; She just wanted a few seconds alone with him.

We could have been so happy, Bernie. She rubbed the smooth wood of the casket.

As she turned to leave, a rogue extension cord from a floor lamp caught her feet and she sprawled onto the coffin, smacking her face hard against it. The spray of roses grazed her head on its way to the floor as the casket started to tip.

"Oh crap, Bernie, get back here." She grabbed the edge of the coffin, but she wasn't strong enough to get it back in place. Her nose was bleeding.

"Can I help you?" A fine specimen of a man in a dark suit was standing behind her.

"Thank you. I had no idea coffins were so heavy."

"Solid oak." He straightened the casket. "You're bleeding. Here, take this tissue. I have a dozen in my pocket. My brother's funeral is about to start and I'll be expected to have enough for everyone."

"Thanks so much. I'm such an idiot." She plucked a rose from her hair.

"You seem a little shaky. Maybe I should walk you out to your car. My name's Byron Newton, by the way."

"Oh, no, really I'm fine. Newton? Well, I do feel a little weak. If I could just hang onto your arm."

*****

KATHLEEN KNOWLES *lives in Middle Cove and is the author of* A Rock And A Hard Place, *a collection of personal essays, and editor of* To Honour the Holiday, *a compilation of Christmas reminiscences from the diaries of Canadian explorers.*

# City of Villainy

## By Christopher Martin

The drizzle trickled down Christian's arms, and then paused for a brief moment at each fingertip before dropping onto the wet sidewalk. He had been standing for some time, arms arched limply outward like an urban scarecrow. The bulk beneath his jacket had made his back ache, but he held position and waited.

It was late evening on Duckworth Street when the fog had crawled in to the spot where Shamus had asked him to wait. This exact spot. Shamus was emphatic about this. And Shamus was a clever man. If Christian needed to stand on this exact spot, well, that's what he was going to do.

Standing like this felt awfully creepy, though. He knew it looked creepy. It wasn't a natural pose. It made him feel nasty in the way that a smile can make you feel nicer.

The rain worked its way down into his socks. The weight beneath his coat was bearing down a little more now. Christian's dark, membranous eyes impatiently searched the dark of the harbour for the promised signal.

\*\*\*

Shamus had saved Christian's life. It was on their third go at robbing the corner store.

Not that they had much success. Each time it had gone wrong in the details. The car would break down. Or the door leading out of the store would jam, holding them up just long enough to get nabbed.

So Shamus started to design little inventions; "gadgets" he called them, "to beat the odds." Like the protractible claw that snatched packs of cigarettes from behind the counter while the clerk's back was turned. The multi-spring clogs that helped them hop suburban fences while on the run. Or the barbecue-briquette-powered engine that pumped homemade "incapacitation gas" into the store. This time Shamus had an old dory waiting harbourside, tied low where it couldn't be seen. They hopped in, pockets full of takings from the Subway cash register, and in the dark they powered up the modified kitchen blenders attached underneath and in "silent mode" made their escape Southside. It was while they were scrambling from the cops along the Southside Hills when Christian slipped on the rocks, hanging helpless while police flashlights flickered overhead like a suburban game of Spotlight. The empty space below eagerly tugged away at his legs.

Shamus could have gotten away but he grabbed Christian's arm and held tight. The mud was slick and the flashlights converged on them as they slid toward the edge.

Later, when Christian's head was being stuffed into the back of the cruiser, one of the cops said that, had he not been taken down for holding up a sandwich shop, Shamus would have gotten a commendation. They didn't find the modified dory.

\*\*\*

By now a police cruiser had pulled up on the sidewalk. Christian kept his gaze downward. He could hear the car door close, followed by the precise steps of the officer.

"All right, Christian, what are you on tonight? Got a call that someone is spooking people. That you? Looks like it."

"I got a right to stand where I wants to."

"And why are you standing like that for? Got a coat hanger stuck in your jacket?"

"It's just the way I likes standing. That's all. Leave me alone. I'm busy."

"Well this is a change of pace. Good. You're about the worst crook I ever heard tell of."

Christian made a rude gesture with one of his raised hands.

"No need to get saucy, now. You can stand how you like, but you shouldn't be standing here anymore. Get moving."

\*\*\*

It was easy to tell that Shamus was the cleverer of the two. While Shamus invented gadgets, Christian preferred to fritter away the day sitting on the steps of Atlantic Place, smoking cigarettes and getting lost in one of the cheap science-fiction paperbacks he'd get from the used bookstore up the road.

He remembered '92, when Shamus' father had bought the sloop from a police repo auction. They'd taken her out into the harbour in the middle of June. It didn't take long for Shamus to figure out how to angle the sail along the tailwind that scrubbed the rocks on The Narrows and spread across the Battery. In summer the wind curled further downtown, perfect for plotting small loops about the harbour. While Shamus worked the rigging, Christian looked out onto the cityscape, splotches of green space and buildings confidently marching downwards to sea level. The Jellybean Rows looked like random bricks from a video game they used to play at the house, Tetris, he remembered it was called. Could he fit the pieces together? He spotted a vertical row; a red, blue, followed by two yellow, just down from the Basilica. He imagined it rotating 90 degrees and dragging slowly down the hill, knocking over stop signs and traffic lights and fitting snugly between two other rows that were separated by an intersection. If he could do that it would be the perfect getaway. Stop chasing cars right in their tracks.

***

The drizzle had stopped. The fog had stretched thin. By now the cruiser had gotten the attention of some pub-goers down the road, arranged in a voyeur's circle.

"Last warning and then I'm going to put you in the lockup for the night. Got it?"

Christian raised his head. The wind had begun to billow underneath the coat, challenging the weight of the waterlogged fabric. His avian eyes picked up the flash of light from the Southside. It was time.

***

The man in the heavy coat stepped back from the crowd. He made one heave of his shoulders, rolling off his coat, which dropped to the ground with a soggy slap. With an audible sigh of relief he stretched his arms downwards and then outwards, revealing a large pair of leather wings, attached to his back via a tangle of straps and buckles. A gust of wind, which had begun in The Narrows, twisted down and then up from the exact spot where he stood. The open wings expanded with ocean air like a pair of great rawhide lungs.

\*\*\*

As he flew over top of the Bowring Building, leaving the crowd behind, Christian carefully shifted his weight with the current and made a large arc over the east docks and toward the Southside Hills. It was foggier up here but he could still make out Shamus' signal. As he approached the cliff he tipped his wings back slightly and glided down onto the bank.

\*\*\*

Shamus watched with pride as his faithful minion executed a perfect landing. He had been focused intently on his handcrafted topographical map of the city. Directional arrows defined all the prevalent air currents; X's marked points of intersection with planned targets. All the details were in place. The city winds were capricious, but they had a pattern. He had not figured out how they could be controlled, not yet, but they could be predicted. All that was required was a little patience and his genius. He gathered his black raincoat and turned away from the map.

"Christian, b'y, I think these cops will have foiled us for the last friggin' time."

\*\*\*\*\*

*CHRISTOPHER MARTIN is a philosopher and writer whose academic work focuses on educational theory and policy. He completed his Phd in London, U.K., and is undertaking a postdoctoral fellowship at Memorial University of Newfoundland. He was born and raised in Newfoundland.*

# Resistance

## By Gerard Collins

I've declared a *fatwa* against pigeons because when they want to nest on your balcony there is no way short of a holy war to stop them.

There are people in St. John's, particularly in the downtown slum district, where pigeons are treated like tribal gods. Misbegotten souls sit on the front stoop and make childish clucking noises with their throats while scattering seeds and crumbs across the sidewalk to attract the flying rodents, which swarm around and make ugly cooing sounds that always make me feel as if I'm in a Hitchcock movie in which the birds will rise up and consume the human species, then in one final, distasteful act of excremental revenge blanket the city in a gooey, white coating. Crows and seagulls also have besieged this town, but it's the pigeons who rule the roost, being plentiful as foot soldiers, superior as kings and dumb as door knockers.

For weeks, I've been shooing them off my apartment balcony on Torbay Road. They land in one of two ways — either manically aflutter as if they'd just undergone a terrible incident and had to pull over to get their emotions in check, or serene and stealthy, barely flapping a wing. These latter ones I despise the most because they seem smarter, as if they were thinking: I'll just sneak in here and stay for a bit, and these stupid humans will never notice. They're looking for a spot to lay their smelly eggs that will ultimately produce hideous vermin offspring. But I won't let them.

Today, as I watched Afghanistan on CNN, a new breed of warrior perched on the railing and peered in through my living room window. "Coo!" he said.

I rushed to the balcony door, like many times before, to shoo him away with a flourish of my straw broom. I've never thumped one, but I always wave the broom like an angry small-town witch defending her porch from impudent urchins.

This time, the invader wasn't falling for my feints. Talons gripping the iron railing, wings tucked ninja-like to his sides, without so much as a self-respecting flinch, he stared back at me with one vulturous eye that reminded me of The Terminator when he gets half his head blown off and yet remains murderously defiant. I knew right then that no matter what I did to banish the commune avis, only one of us could win this battle, and the pigeon intended to be that victor.

"Get outta here!" I yelled. "Get your own home!"

The offensive bird blinked at me, causing me to raise my broom and take a preemptive swipe at his overstuffed little body. I peered nervously over the balcony to the sidewalk below to make sure PETA hadn't sent a decoy to frame me for animal abuse. Still, it was in my favour that I had thus far resisted from striking him.

The pigeon morphed into survival mode by spreading his wings, which caught the sun's beam and radiated a panoply of sparkling violet, emerald and indigo flecks against the otherwise dull gray camouflage provided by its feathers. A tiny white puff fluttered towards my face and planted itself on my lips, sending me into a sputter like an accidental swimmer who had nearly drowned. Unharmed and oblivious, the bird merely repositioned himself.

"Go on!" I screamed, and I again I tilted my broom in his vicinity. Once more, he spread his wings, posted a glorious display of colour and parachuted onto my railing, peering at me with his Terminator eye and uttering a single word: "Coo!"

I was about to leap forward and wring its puny feathered throat when a knock came on the living room door. PETA, I assumed. Tromping to the door, I expected to see Pamela Anderson in a T-shirt and cutoff jeans, standing there with handcuffs dangling. But it turned out to be two Jehovah's Witnesses in black suits and ties, looking like the Men in Black. While I stood gaping at them, trying to figure out which movie I'd seen them in, they asked me if I'd given any thought to the state of the world and whether I believed in Jesus.

"That depends," I said. "Does Jesus have wings?"

The one who'd spoken glanced at the other one and, without blinking, continued to sermonize, while the other tried to force a copy of The Watchtower into my fisted hands. I resisted by claiming to have read it already. "Give it to someone who needs it."

"Everyone needs Jesus," said the shorter, forceful one.

"If he can get the pigeons off my balcony, I'd be much obliged. 'Cause right now, I've got a crusade that needs tending." While they were pondering my pronouncement, I closed the door.

By the time I got back to the balcony door, the pigeon had invited his wife — or maybe his commanding officer, for all I knew — and they were both standing on the rail, cooing conspiratorially as if deciding whether my place was better than the last condo they'd viewed, or whether they should keep looking for something more in their price range. But since they were freeloading, the price seemed to be about right. They both looked at me with their beady little eyes, and they shook their sun-glinted feathers like a negotiating shrug, and, in perfect harmony spoke exactly the same word: "Coo!"

I swung my broom at them, intending to harm. But they were quicker than me and flew off just enough to fall out of my reach while floating on the air like descending archangels with an important message for mankind, or just me.

Again, I struck, with the intent of maiming or, if necessary, killing them. Again, they flew off and alit, a thrust and parry effect that the three of us repeated several more times before I finally clipped one wing and the wounded aviator plummeted to my balcony floor. As the other one attacked me, I hoisted the broom to defend myself. He came at me, talons up and beak wide open as if to say, "You killed my companion and now you must die!"

Fearful of gaining a bird in the house, I ended the siege by slamming the door shut amid the sound and fury of futile flapping. When I lifted the blind and peered out, the attacking bird had abandoned his aggression and stood over the body of his fallen compadre, strutting and blinking. "Coo!" it said, then said it again: "Coo! Coo!"

Until finally, the fallen one opened one little dark eye and uttered the cry of never surrender: "Coo!"

Together, they flew off as if neither had been injured — at least not physically.

Only when I saw them depart in that way, one looking after the other, crying out their message or warning or whatever it was, did I think upon the two Witnesses and whether they were still standing outside my living room door, ready to resume my interrogation.

I didn't check.

But I knew they'd be back.

*****

GERARD COLLINS *is a St. John's-based writer, originally from Bond's Path, Placentia. He has won several awards for fiction, including the Percy Janes First Novel Award. His first book, a short-story collection called* Moonlight Sketches, *was published by Killick Press in April 2011.*

# The Star of the Sea

## By Lisa Porter

The smell of damp wood hits Sally as she rounds the corner on Duckworth Street to turn up Bates Hill. The inevitability of decay kept at bay for so long with oil paint and oil heat now let loose. Earth reclaims her own every time. The Hall that beckoned sailors for 90 years was headless. Open air had already replaced the mansard roof. Its secrets released into the ether. Four colonial pillars out of work with nothing to hold. She thinks it unseemly to be seen like that. Stripped naked, empty sockets gaping where windows had been, vapour barrier flapping in the wind. They don't tear down buildings with wrecking balls like you see on television. No *Koyaanisqatsi* splendour. No soundtrack crescending to a portentous sublime. No. This was a slow, methodical dismantling on a human scale. A disenchanting. The Star of the Sea is coming down.

What was it she was seeing? Was it a wedding? A birthday? God, it must be 20 years. She can see her aunt Vivian holding a scarlet-cheeked toddler splayed in deep sleep on her lap. A mass of yellow curls plastered flat against the boy's forehead wet with sweat. The heat of the dance hall rippled as the bass rhythm vibrated up through the floor into their bodies. Vivian radiated that aura of casual authority found in those unburdened by idle self-consciousness. She thought insecurity an appalling waste of energy and could not understand why people succumbed to it. It was self-indulgent, a kind of greed in its own way, this cloying need to be assured by others. The child in her arms, her second grandchild, feared nothing — a gift of genes bestowed with easy benevolence. Sally's genes came from some other line in the family. The one mired in doubt and indecision.

She turns away, pushing down the wave of sticky nostalgia and makes her way up the road to where she has parked, being careful not to send the door crashing into the car downhill from her. This is something you learn young in St. John's. Gravity is a demanding companion, always pulling you down to sea level where the air is thick and cool, protecting you from the lightheadedness of excessive heights. She starts the car and drives home.

Sally's neighbour, Frank, lived somewhere in the Caribbean for a long time before he came home. Home to roost. In his front garden, Frank has a canopy under which he houses a barbecue, a round picnic table, some chairs and a bamboo bar. He comes home from work and cooks up jerk chicken every day in the summer, sometimes fish. He chats with the tourists on their way to Quidi Vidi. The boom box plays *Besame Mucho*. Kiss me. Kiss me a lot. His skin is a deep ruddy brown. A perma-tan, Vivian would have called it. Vivian didn't believe in sunbathing. She lost her best friend every winter to Florida, and then to cancer. Sally reminded Vivian that it was lung cancer, not skin cancer — that it was the forty years of Export A's, but that didn't wash with Vivian. It was that goddamn sun, she said. It ruined her skin, dried her up like a prune, swallowed her whole. "Stay out of the sun, Sally," she would say, "and you will bloom like an English rose." Yes, thinks Sally, prickly.

She pulls into the driveway and waves to Frank. Today he's barbecuing salmon on a cedar plank. The smell makes her think of the gerbils or guinea pigs or whatever it was her cousins had when they were growing up. Why would you want your fish to taste like a rodent cage? Who came up with that idea? Someone makes a lot of money selling cedar planks in grocery stores. Sally knew there were many things in the world she would never understand. Why couldn't she think of something so simple that would make her rich? She considers the idea of envy, which is different from jealousy, although contemporary usage confuses the two. You feel envy towards someone who possesses something that you would like to have — wealth or beauty or wit. It is closely associated with covetousness. On the other hand you feel jealousy when you are the person in possession of something — love comes to mind — and fear losing it to another. Jealousy akin to zealot, the Greek word for those passionately adherent to a cause. Sally doesn't like the feeling of envy. It is childish, immature. It is the stuff of situation comedies. It is the most tedious of human conditions.

Aunt Vivian would have scoffed at Sally's self-analysis. Envy, jealousy — all the deadly sins are simply part of the human condition. She loved every one of them like her own children. Don't be such a frigging puritan. Do you think you're so different from everyone else? Sally ignores the voice in her head, concentrating on her goal to cultivate *mudita*, the Buddhist term for finding joy in the success of others. Instead she thinks of mojito, a Cuban drink made of rum and sugar and mint. Frank waves back.

In Morocco, goats climb argan trees to eat their nuts. Sally saw a photo in a National Geographic magazine. Eight shaggy brown goats stand on the branches of a scraggly tree. It look like a child's sticker book in which a small child had placed stickers of the goats incorrectly in the tree instead of on the ground. The argan nut has been used by the Berbers for thousands of years as food, skin nourishment and medicine. Now Sally's hairdresser sells it to her. Sally feels sad for the goats, knowing that their next meal is now going to make her hair shiny. Aunt Viv would have said shag the goats. Shag your sadness. Shag it all.

Sally sits in the car for a long time until Frank finally comes over and asks if she is all right.

"Yes," she says, "I'm fine. My aunt died."

"I'm so sorry."

"It's okay, thanks. She was 92."

"I got a salmon on the grill."

"Do you have any rum?"

Frank nods.

Sally gets out of the car and brushes back her hair.

"I'll get the soda."

*****

*LISA PORTER is a filmmaker and performer living in St. John's.*

# A Bone In France

## By David C. Kennedy

The other visitors and the tour guide had moved on to another section of the memorial site with their digital cameras and improvised reverence. I was tired and sat in a trench where the Newfoundland soldiers had huddled just before they went over the top to face the German machine guns here in Beaumont Hamel on July 1, 1916. My stumps were sore and raw from chafing against my titanium legs, courtesy of a Taliban IED two years ago near Kabul. I still couldn't believe what had happened and was hoping to wake up soon from a very bad dream.

I wasn't sure why I had come on this tour of the Somme with a large group of Newfoundlanders and a bunch of couples from Labrador City. Maybe I thought I could then understand and possibly accept what had happened to me in Afghanistan if I could get somehow connected to the spirits of the young lads from the coves and bays at home, lying here beneath me. They who had been slaughtered on orders from some British officer, suffering from unbridled enthusiasm and ambition. Leaning on my hands, I squirmed my backside around trying to get more comfortable and as I did I felt something under my right hand. I dug a little and pulled up a dirty pale-grey bone. I shuddered when I realized I was holding a piece of a young Newfoundland soldier who had probably been shot to bits by a German gun. My knowledge of human anatomy was meagre and I didn't know what bone it was, but it had a deep groove in it. I guessed it had been made by a German bullet flying through the French air like a death sentence from hell. I got up and moved away to another spot and sat down again because I didn't want to sit atop the remains of a fellow Newfoundlander, decades removed notwithstanding.

I had heard that most of the boys here at Beaumont Hamel had died quickly and I hoped it was so. I had prayed many times to die quickly as well, instead of having to endure the ravages of recovery after Afghanistan, or Satan's playground, as a buddy of mine called it. I held the bone in my hand and tried to feel some spiritual or psychic vibrations from it, some message of wisdom or comfort for me. The only thing that happened was that I suddenly recalled bits of a poem my great-grandmother had written about her husband who had also died here in these acres of horror, in cerements of mud and blood. I couldn't recall all of her poem, only this:

*Nighttime and a lonely heart,*

*shit-baked he got.*

*Up in the morning he got,*

*over the top he got,*

*something in the air he got,*

*a German bullet he got,*

*just above his web belt he got.*

*Dead he got.*

*A hug and a whisper I got.*

I also remembered that in the aftermath of that July day, when the world was filled with praise and sorrow for the young men of the Royal Newfoundland Regiment who had been sent to their deaths as fast as an ammunition belt feeds death to a machine gun, a Major-General Sir Beauvoir De Lisle said about the squandered men that their assault failed only because dead men can advance no further. I felt great rage again, as I often had in the last few years, over the wasted limbs and lives of all wars. I'd like to re-name this place The Field of Squander.

There was only silence and small birds here now. It's funny, I thought, but birds never go to war. They never form regiments. They have no weapons and, as far as I know, not one bird in history has ever had a titanium limb. So what is it they know that humans do not? They eat, sleep, build nests, have baby birds and teach them how to eat, sleep, and build nests, and then continue. Without a single platoon. Without a single weapon. They sleep without the death of another on their conscience and they do not grieve. Like me.

I was grieving for myself and now, for these young heroes on whose bones I sat and pondered. Since my injuries I have tried to find solace in many ways, even in booze. Nothing helped. I tried to find comfort in the wisdom of the wise. Kahlil Gibran's *The Prophet*, for example. His line about pain still haunts me: *And he said: Your pain is the breaking of the shell that encloses your understanding.* No understanding ever came from his words but I did find clarity in American songwriter Tom Paxton's song *When Princes Meet*, especially his lines: *When kings make war, the poor little men must fight them. They must do more. They hold out their necks for great lord's swords to bite them.*

My rage accepted these words and in recalling them I accomplished nothing. I thought of my little nephew, nine years old, pale, delicate limbs, as fragile as a cobweb. What war was he being prepared for, I wondered.

I glanced over at the others who were all busy taking pictures of each other and in groups with the Beaumont Hamel monuments in the background. For some reason it reminded me of a Japanese couple I had met once at the base of the Matterhorn in Switzerland. They had asked me to take their picture with one of the many cameras they had slung over their shoulders. I agreed and was astonished when they asked me to take the picture with their hotel behind them and not the spectacular mountain. I'm not a stupid person but their logic missed my skull by about six inches.

I studied the bone for a while. How many unrequited dreams were contained in its DNA? How many joys in its long ago desiccated marrow? Had he seen a young girl blush? Had she made him clumsy? Given him a mouthful of inane tongues? Had he already held his own disarticulated babe in his arms? By the time he had had his first military pay and pinned on the shiny brass caribou, the emblem of the Royal Newfoundland Regiment, had it already been too late for the *Deus Miseratur*, the *Psalm of Mercy*?

So why did we do it in Gallipoli, the Somme, the Pacific, Korea, Afghanistan and elsewhere? Maybe we did it because we didn't know how not to.

I rolled the old bone around in my hands.

"See you soon, my brother-in-arms."

I pushed the bone back into the earth as far as I could, and started to weep.

*****

DAVID C. KENNEDY *was a university professor in South Korea from 1995-2010. Before that he was a TV/radio journalist in Newfoundland and Labrador, and director of Hansard in the Newfoundland and Labrador legislature. He lives in Conception Bay South.*

# Merrymeeting

## By Danielle Devereaux

When they were building the new Sobeys on Merrymeeting Road and the site was fenced with white sheets of plywood, someone wrote the word Sobeys with a line through each S on the fence — $OBEY$ — in black permanent marker. Anna thinks of it now, standing in the green space at the edge of the Sobeys parking lot.

The store is squat, rectangular, a triangle peak over each entrance. It's a style that reminds Anna of toy blocks, Fisher Price. If giants play Monopoly, they use game pieces like this. The Sobeys sign above the main entrance glows bright green. It was clever, the $OBEY$ marking. Anna wonders if one of the volunteers at Heavenly Creatures might have written it. The ones she's met all seem clever like that. Clever and soft-hearted and brave. It's the kind of thing they would've protested — a big box store planking its arse down on a soccer field. Corporate greed.

Anna stopped shopping at Sobeys years ago, after they built that store on the old Mount Cashel property. Driving past the orphanage, the rolling fields of green and mature trees, used to feel like catching a glimpse of another world — as if a piece of the Bronte sisters' England had fallen onto Elizabeth Avenue. She could understand why people wanted the building torn down, it was stately and grand, but yes of course, tear it down so the men who'd been boys in that horrible place never had to see it again. But not the trees. Another box shop, a pool of asphalt, wouldn't give any boy back his childhood. When council approved the build, after some but not enough protest, Anna wrote a letter to Sobeys' head office saying that from now on she would shop elsewhere. She cut her Sobeys card into strips, put it all in an envelope. They'd written back a polite, vague letter valuing her opinion. Her own letter had also been polite. In those days Anna felt it was important to always be polite.

The new Sobeys has actually been on Merrymeeting Road for almost a decade; Anna still doesn't shop there. Though she does sometimes, especially lately, shop at the liquor store attached to it.

Sobeys cannot own the liquor store, which must still belong to the Liquor Corporation, but it is part of the same building that ate the soccer field, and she's not proud of this bend in her stance. She also walks her dog around the green perimeter of the store's parking lot, which is why she is standing there now, staring at the glowing green of the Sobeys sign, remembering the clever $OBEY$.

If someone were to throw a rock or a brick, something heavy, at the S's now, if the lights broke, the green letters would glow "obey." Anna would like to see this, a glowing green "obey" on Merrymeeting Road. Not that Anna is a vandal (the Sobeys card she shredded had, after all, been her own); she is not some young punk. Anna is 53 and has always obeyed the rules — paid parking tickets if she inadvertently let a meter run out, followed speed limits. She has obeyed social rules, too: married, two kids, a house, a job. And she'd not been unhappy with this situation, she did not mind following these rules. If she is remembering correctly, she'd thought that the rules were quite all right.

Then her daughter Gillian got married and six months later Anna's husband said he was leaving. He'd fallen in love with someone else. He didn't mean for it to happen, but it did, and he was sorry, and he left Anna for Gillian's childhood best friend. She'd been a bridesmaid in the wedding party. Maid of honour.

Anna starts to laugh, except the laugh gets caught in a tangle and comes out more like a sob.

If she'd read it in a novel, some foolish chick-lit thing that her sister-in-law picked out for book club, she would've dismissed the storyline as ridiculous, unbelievable. Why would a 28-year-old woman want anything to do with her girlfriend's 55-year-old father? What kind of father would have an affair with, leave the mother of his children for, his daughter's best friend? A girl he'd known since she was a little kid playing pass-the-parcel at birthday parties, squished, alongside his own daughter, behind Gillian's bed, making all the stuffed toys in the room perform some silly play about bears and cats and Cabbage Patch Kids. Jesus.

Anna's shoulders shake. This is why she has started to walk only at night. She is prone to fits of sobbing laughter, to cursing to herself, quietly, but aloud, to an anger that boils up from the hollows of her hip bones, clenching her jaw shut so tight she might well splinter her own teeth. One hand over her mouth, eyes blurry and wet, Anna holds her breath until whatever it is that's clutched in her throat lets go and she has to haul in gaping lungfuls of air.

Anna's husband is allergic to dogs. She adopted Hank 10 weeks after he left. She'd always wanted a dog, but now she needed one. She needs to walk. If she doesn't walk, fast, for hours at a time, a blood vessel in her brain will surely burst; but didn't she always tell her daughter that it's not safe at night, even in this small city, for a woman to be walking alone? When she called Heavenly Creatures she told them she was looking for a big dog, a dog that liked to be walked. They said Hank had come from Labrador. A Husky-Lab cross, he must've lived outdoors in Labrador, but his foster family said it had taken him no time to get used to living indoors. They said he was never any trouble — no accidents on the carpet, no torn sofas. Hank seems entirely suited to his new big city-life, to walking alongside Anna on a retractable leash, sleeping at the foot of her queen-sized bed, ignore a patch of sunlight on the tiled kitchen floor.

Hank is a good dog. Calm. He looks back at Anna as she swallows chunks of air, walks toward her, presses the side of his face to her thigh. Anna strokes the thick fur at the top of his head, tries to calm her breathing. She's been doing yoga classes, and the instructor, who is young and pretty and kind, is big on intentional breathing. "We must always remember," Melanie says, "how important it is to breathe." Anna breathes. Breathing helps. She looks into Hank's beautiful dog blue eyes and smiles. Smiling helps. The dog and walking all over St. John's at all hours of the night help. And she can see now that throwing something, throwing something heavy, fast and hard, the sound of splintering glass, bursting lights, would help too.

*****

*DANIELLE DEVEREAUX'S poetry and non-fiction writing have appeared in a variety of Canadian publications. An alumnus of the Banff Writing Studio, her poetry manuscript-in-progress was short-listed for the 2009 Fresh Fish Award for Emerging Writers. She lives in St. John's.*

# Firebug

## By Beth Ryan

As soon as the singer hops up onto the stage, I am there. I start to bounce on my toes a little like a boxer getting ready for a fight. The crack of the drumsticks is the band's cue to start their first song and mine to shimmy to the dance floor. I stake out my space by spinning in ever-widening circles, my long hair whirling like helicopter blades. The vibrations in the floor tickle my feet. I am blanketed in rhythm and melody. And I dance. All the local bands know me. The front man will sometimes give me a wink before he gets started.

This one's for Edie! C'mon everybody, don't leave her up there all alone. Dance!

I never intended to become a sideshow that everyone expects when a band plays at the Rose and Thistle or the Spur or the Ship. But some people only know me as that girl who dances by herself. What's the alternative? It's not very often that a guy will come over and jerk his thumb towards the dance floor and give you a wink that says you've been chosen. And I don't travel with a group of girls, a ready-made troupe of dance partners who jump to their feet with a shriek when their favourite song starts. So I just do my own thing. I dance with myself.

My mistake was letting Harlow in on it.

*** 

Harlow tells Garth that he would not be able to make it to the wedding. "Sorry, Dad," he said, "I just can't swing it. I've got this wicked job planting trees in British Columbia." Meanwhile, Harlow and my mother came up with a clever plan to get him here as a surprise for Garth. The clueless bridegroom is at the airport now, searching the arrivals area for a fictitious aunt flying in from Ottawa.

The front door slams. In comes Garth with a duffle bag slung over one shoulder. He's a long, lanky man who seems to fold and unfold himself like one of those wooden rulers that are hinged every 12 inches. His face is similarly long — a cross between the farmer with the pitchfork in the *American Gothic* painting and that syrupy pop singer with the long hair. Michael Bolton? Yeah, him. But without the long hair. The length of Garth's face makes him seem irrevocably sad but today, his smile has rearranged his features into a more pleasing combination.

"So here I was ... looking for Jeannie's aunt and look who I find!"

Garth steps aside to beckon Harlow into the room. He is tall like Garth and similarly slim. But nothing else is the same. White skin, big brown eyes, a fringe of shaggy hair that's as red as a brand new penny. He has a face that makes you want to look.

My mother heads for Harlow, her arm opens.

"Finally, I get to meet you," she says. "Welcome."

He ducks down to meet her hug and kisses her cheek.

My mother waves me over.

"Edie, this is your soon-to-be new stepbrother, Harlow."

"Hey," I say.

"Hey, Edie."

Good to see we're keeping it low-key. No need for hugs and gushing. We're strangers, not family. And even if he was my real long-lost brother arriving home from some dangerous adventure in the jungle, I would not start wailing and throwing my arms around him. I like everything kept on an even keel. If it doesn't get really high, then it doesn't have to go really low afterwards.

"This is so exciting," my mother tells Harlow. "Edie always wanted a big brother."

"Well, I'm glad I showed up after all these years," Harlow says. He smirks like he's got something on me.

"Well," Garth says, "Harlow is pretty stoked about getting a new family, too. Aren't you, Harlow?"

He grins in response.

"Dad is right. I'm so stoked about this. You don't even know!"

My mother and Garth beam at us as if we've just performed in a school play.

"Harlow here is a musician. He's a pretty mean guitar player," Garth offers.

"Edie knows all of the local bands," my mother counters. "She could introduce you to them!"

Soon I have agreed to take Harlow with me when I go out that night to see a band.

***

It's been two weeks since the wedding and it seems Harlow has become my sidekick, inviting himself along on my late-night jaunts to the bars. He dances near me, around me, behind me, beside me. But never with me. But I can feel him there even when I can't see him. When we're not dancing, he is flitting through the crowd, stopping to greet every woman he brushes against. His hands linger on their shoulders and backs and hips, his mouth grazes their cheeks as he leans in to whisper to them. He loves talking to strangers, making them his friends.

He tells me that he has decided to rent a room downtown.

"You never know, I may decide to extend my stay in your friendly little town."

"Aren't we the lucky ones?" I say. "So where will you live?"

"You remember Martina from the other night?"

Oh, I remember Martina. Harlow's new friend. She just showed up in town a while ago, from nowhere in particular, offers no details, shares nothing. And people just can't get enough of her. That's something for my to-do list — be more mysterious. Harlow introduced me to her at a party.

"Hello Edith," she said, taking my hand in hers and kissing my cheek. "You are Harlow's little sister."

"Not exactly," I say. "It's Edie actually."

"Ah," Martina nodded, "I see."

"Well," Harlow says, "Martina is looking for a roommate."

"Good for you," I say, but the thought of him living with mysterious Martina leaves me shivery.

The only time I visit the apartment, I find them in the living room. Martina is lying on the couch, her feet in Harlow's lap. They smoke a joint, Harlow leaning the length of Martina's legs to pass it to her, one hand on her thigh.

"Hello Edith," Martina says, in a dreamy voice, her eyelids barely open. She persists in calling me that, giving my full name a vaguely menacing undertone.

***

Just when I thought I couldn't bear the idea of Harlow sleeping in that apartment for one more minute, the building goes up in flames. Whoosh. I stand on the south side of Duckworth Street, trembling in my raincoat. The rain falls so hard and fast that it seems impossible for the fire to resist. But it does, flames dancing out the windows of Harlow's bedroom. Fire shoots straight up from the roof into the dark sky. I see Harlow snake through the crowd and make his way to me.

"You're okay," I say, but I knew he was not at home.

He stands next to me and takes my hand. I look up into Harlow's face and it is glowing in the firelight, tiny fires flickering in the dark part of his eyes.

"It's just so beautiful," Harlow says, as his few belongings are being incinerated.

*****

BETH RYAN *is a lifelong townie. Her first book of short stories,* What Is Invisible, *won the John and Margaret Savage first book award for Atlantic Canadian writers in 2004. She's been trying to write her first novel ever since. It's still not finished.*

# The Space in Between

## By Sharon Bala

Your name is Allan Dowden and you are born to a fisherman called William and his wife Susannah during the middle years of Queen Victoria's reign[1]. You are an Englishman by birth, a Newfoundlander by death and the years in between are spent within a small radius on a large island.

You grow up in a blue house on Mullock Street[2] among a gaggle of siblings and cousins, all flailing limbs and open mouths and leaking noses. The cousin Dowdens live in a mirror-image house next door. The walls are paper thin. When the cousins on one side burst into impromptu song, the cousins on the other pick up the chorus. On Sundays there are hymns and turnip peels.

This neighbourhood of close-set chimney pots is perched on the edge of the city limits and empties into an open field where your childhood disappears in a blur of skinned knees and tousled hair, ill-suppressed whispers carried by the wind. The field is a vast ocean that shrinks as you expand.

After a time, there is a girl. You take her skating on a frozen pond. She is unsteady and falls often. Though her lip trembles, she does not cry. You feel simultaneously protective and proud.

The wedding is held on a Tuesday in July. Your bride wears blue silk and a dainty white hat.[3] Marriage brings solace. You move out of the boisterous blue house — still inhabited by your mother, two grown brothers and a sister[4] — and into a newly built two storey on Circular Road. The smell of hops from the brewery at the end of the street hangs low with the fog. You are a mason for Harvey and Co.[5] Your bride is soft-spoken. On Sundays, she takes a little sugar in her tea. Before she climbs in, you lie on her side of the bed to

---

[1] St. Thomas' Anglican Baptism Records 1867-1875
[2] McAlpines Directory 1894
[3] St. John's Daily News, July 21, 1909
[4] McAlpines Directory, 1908
[5] McAlphines Directory, 1913

warm it up. She makes partridgeberry pie and serves you the biggest slice.

Your duo becomes a trio. Her name is Phyllis and she arrives in March with a blizzard that enfolds the city in a white cocoon. Tiny fingernails grow on lengthening limbs until it is her turn to race through fields of long grass, too big to sit on her father's shoulders and stare up at the endless shelves of biscuit tins at Murphy's Grocery. One day while inspecting tomatoes at the market, your mother clutches her head and dies.

It is your turn next. A tightening in the chest, a twitch, a twinge, and suddenly there is a doctor called McPhearson.[6] He warms the stethoscope in the crook of his arm and delivers the news as kindly as possible: you are dead.

In a cemetery on a hill overlooking a lake you lie alongside your compatriots.[7] A name and two years with a space in between. The space in which all the comedies and tragedies took place. All the victories and defeats, the heartbeats and deep breaths, the gentle sighs and troubled groans. The turnip peels and hymns; the smell of hops and partridgeberry pie; the tiny fingernails. All the miscellaneous moments that make up a life.

*****

*SHARON BALA is a transplanted mainlander living in St. John's. Her work has appeared in The Globe and Mail and This Great Society. A spin doctor by trade, she pens fiction in stolen moments and is studiously ignoring a half-written novel in the hopes that it will finish itself.*

---

[6] Obituary, Daily News, July 1923
[7] Anglican Cemetery, coordinates 47 degrees 34.49 north by 52 degrees 41.97 west.

# Blue Balloons

### By Alan W. Davidson

Sanjeev Doyle lay in the dirt.

He was partially shaded by a tall, yellow birch. The tree was once the pride of Ochre Pit Cove, however a recent storm had snapped off its largest branch and the relentless heat had caused the remaining leaves to grow brittle. The boy spied a black fly feeding on his arm and he squat it, leaving a bloody smear in the fine, dark hair.

Neatly arranged in the scorching sun was a row of balloons and several empty bean tins. Lima beans, wax beans and string beans. He loathed them all equally.

A single crow, near the top of the tree, cackled at the boy.

Sanjeev stood up and picked at the tree's bark with his dirty finger nail. He snapped a twig from the lowest branch, held it to his nose and breathed in its wintergreen scent. He was reminded of Grandfather Ravi's visit from Mumbai last summer. Naa-naa-jee had discovered that wearing long underwear and two sweaters made the Newfoundland weather nearly tolerable. The boy and his grandfather spent long hours wandering the wooded trails in the hills west of the village. The old man had been a science teacher and took great joy in imparting knowledge to his only grandson.

Grandfather Ravi had given the boy a slingshot and carefully instructed him on its use, just as *his* grandfather had taught him years before. Eventually, though, the old man returned home as autumn's colours bled into winter's desolation.

One night, several weeks ago, the choppy water of Conception Bay was illuminated by a series of bright flashes that shimmered and danced on the horizon. The sky above St. John's glowed amber and crimson for a long time and the air reeked of smoke and metal.

Sanjeev's parents had both worked as physicians in Carbonear.

They had left him alone with a cache of food and told him they were driving to town for a few days to give assistance. At first the neighbours dropped in to check on the boy. In the morning, Mr. Boland and his dog stopped by to see that he ate breakfast. In the evening, Mrs. Oliver helped him to prepare supper. Eventually, though, they both fell ill and stopped visiting, forcing Sanjeev to fend for himself. Like a thief, he crept into the saltbox houses of the village and emptied their pantries of tinned food. Over time he grew accustomed to the sights, and the smells, of his silent neighbours.

The village food supply was nearly exhausted and the only living creatures he had seen for days were the flies that constantly tormented him. Even Mr. Boland's crackie had stopped coming by for food. Sanjeev visited the houses for a final time and carted off the remaining tins of evil beans. The boy had also found a bag of balloons in a kitchen drawer. He knew it was near his birthday but he had lost track of the days and could not be sure.

He blew up several blue balloons and carefully placed one between each of the empty tins. Sanjeev accomplished this by tying a bit of string to each balloon and using push-pins to fasten them to scraps of wood. A breeze now swept across the barren landscape, causing the balloons to bounce about at the ends of their tethers.

Sanjeev wiped his sweaty palms down the front of his jeans and snatched a stone from the pile at his feet. He felt its rough edges with his fingertips and then placed it in the leather pouch of the slingshot. The boy pulled back the tubing, took aim at the first tin and released. The stone flew from his slingshot and he heard a hollow "thunk" as the tin spiraled backwards from the impact. His second stone popped the adjacent balloon. He continued along the line of targets in a vain attempt to distract himself from the pains cramping his stomach. The wind grew stronger, whipping about the final balloon. Sanjeev took aim and fired. He missed. Again he tried, but the stone merely glanced off the rubber target.

"Your shooting, my boy, has lost its edge." Sanjeev whirled about at the sound of the familiar voice.

"Who is there? What do you want?" The leaves of the birch whispered quietly in response and the crow continued to mock him.

"Try again, young master! Never give up!" Sanjeev looked back to the remaining target.

Encased within the blue balloon was the face of Naa-naa-jee, resembling Lord Vishnu himself.

"What is wrong, boy?"

"You are ... dead."

"Yes, perhaps. As are most—"

"Then you cannot be talking to me."

"Why not? I still have a working mouth and one or two lessons to teach," he said. The azure face smiled and wobbled back and forth with the breeze.

"You cannot teach me!"

"Do not be too proud to be told, insolent boy! Solutions are very often simple, their revelation most obvious."

"I have no time for riddles. Leave me alone, you bloody ghost!"

"Ha! A ghost am I? Remember what I taught you, Sanjeev. Hold your breath for a moment, just before you release your stone."

"Go to hell, you demon!" Sanjeev shouted.

"My boy ... perhaps we are already there." The visage closed its eyes and bellowed laughter toward several white birds circling high in the cloudless sky.

Sanjeev took aim and fired his final stone. It popped the last balloon and the flaccid rubber fell to the dirt. The boy curled into a ball, hid his face in the crook of his arm and cried until sleep released him from his burden.

When he awoke, Sanjeev discovered a large seagull poking at one of the empty bean tins with its long beak. The boy snaked his fingers to his pocket and removed a steel ball bearing. He pinched it in the pouch and quickly stretched back the rubber tubing. Sanjeev let the tubing go slack. The boy closed his eyes for a moment and slowly pulled the tubing tight. He held his breath, aimed and then released the heavy ball. It struck the bird on its side and sent it sprawling in a flurry of squawks and feathers.

Sanjeev leaped to his feet and shouted, punching the air with a small, brown fist. He began to gather scraps of wood to build a fire.

Tonight he would eat meat.

*****

*ALAN W. DAVIDSON has lived in St. John's for five years and has completed creative writing courses in London, Ont., and at Memorial University. He is a member of the Writers' Alliance of Newfoundland and Labrador.*

# The Victrola

## By Michael Finn

During his voyage to New York City early in the fall of 1920, the merchant Levi Jenkins of Fox Cove had gone into Macy's department store and bought a wonderful machine.

The machine was not much to look at: just a rectangular box of polished dark wood standing on four short legs, with a crank jutting from one side at the top, and a set of double doors in the front. It was about as high as a man's waist.

The wonder of this object was not immediately apparent, and the men who unloaded it from Mr. Jenkins' boat and took it by cart up the path to his house under the brow of the hill did not fully understand the solicitude with which Mr. Jenkins supervised the transfer. Were it not for the oddity of the crank, they would have thought it was another expensive ornamental cabinet for Mrs. Jenkins. Only after they had set it in front of the open parlour window was the wonder of it revealed.

"Now, b'ys," said Mr. Jenkins, "Ye've got to stay a bit and listen to me new Victrola."

He raised the lid of the box to reveal a strange mechanism, the like of which the shy guests had never seen before; it consisted mostly of a large plate with a nub of a spindle in the very centre, and a curved, tapering, tubular silver arm attached to a metal pivot.

He crouched down and opened first the topmost, smaller set of double doors, and then the larger bottom ones.

The latter enclosed a storage cabinet, from which Mr. Jenkins took a shiny black disc. It was about the same diameter as the plate at the top of the machine, and in its middle was a small hole. He carefully centred this hole over the spindle and gently laid the disc on the plate. Then, very deliberately, he turned the crank several times, and when he released it the plate began to spin. Next, using thumb and forefinger, he eased the silver arm from its cradle, swung it slowly over the spinning disc, and delicately placed its needle tip on the outermost edge.

Turning to them, Mr. Jenkins held up his finger. Like a preacher admonishing his congregants to be attentive, he said: "Now just listen. This is the great Caruso. 'Tis a song in praise of the Virgin Mary. 'Tis almost like a prayer. *Ave Maria* 'tis called. By an Austrian, a fella named Schubert."

At first they heard a faint crackling hiss, like the whisper of surf sliding down a sandy beach on a still night, or the venting of steam from a junk of green wood on a bed of hot embers. But then the strangest, most wonderful thing of all occurred. The hissing subsided and gave way to a sweet, singing note that surged and grew until it expanded into the sinuous, shivery line of a solo violin, and so startled were they by its clarity that for a moment they ceased to wonder at the obvious but nonetheless astonishing connection between the music and the spinning black disc.

If the top of the Victrola had been closed and the music had continued to flow from the box, they might have imagined an elfin violinist imprisoned inside it, playing for his release.

But then something even more wonderful happened. Accompanying the violinist was a voice the like of which no one in Fox Cove had ever heard before. And it was only when they heard this voice, whose purity and power no singer they knew of could dream of matching, that they realized who the great Caruso was. At first they had thought that perhaps the violinist was Caruso. But no ... no; clearly, it was the singer. For as marvellous as the violin sounded to ears attuned to the shrieks of gulls or the wails of widows or the murmurs of prayers on stormy nights, the singing of this voice soared above the singing of the violin, absorbing and subduing it, and it was as if the great Caruso were standing on top of a high hill and filling the space below with the voice of a god come down from the heights of the moon.

And although they could not comprehend the words he sang, they knew he sang of something for which he must have ached with reverence and gratitude, for the power of the voice was tempered with humility and awe. It was the reverence a person might feel as he watched the sea and sky on a stormy day, knowing he was in the presence of an element that only God Himself could tame.

A current of warm air from the garden wafted through the window. The curtains flickered. The voice of Caruso mingled with the scent of grass and wild roses and the odour of the sea. It drifted out the window and through the garden. As it soared over the wild-rose hedge it filled the air over the bank that sloped towards the village. In the stillness of the afternoon the voice pervaded the amphitheatre of the rocky hills enclosing the harbour. It penetrated every nook and cranny, stole through windows and doors left open to welcome the warmth. Heads turned. Faces peered from windows. Children paused at play, and as old men napped on the settle in the afternoon warmth, the singing suffused their dreams and lured them into a dwall in which they tossed and sighed and wondered if they had died and entered Paradise. Over the stillness of the black harbour the voice drifted and circled until it escaped through the rocky notch of the harbour entry. It echoed from the hills and mingled with the shrieks of gulls and terns until it dwindled and disappeared in the cool briny mist floating over the surface of the sea.

The music faded into the soft ember-crackle. Mr. Jenkins picked up the silver arm, which had glided towards the spindle in the centre of the disc, and returned it to its cradle.

"Now b'ys," he said. "Weren't that the most wonderful voice you ever did hear? Weren't it?"

And yes, they said, indeed it were the most wonderful voice that they ever did hear.

Years later, long after the Victrola, its mahogany finish dulled and scratched from neglect, had been stowed in the back of the shed in Mr. Jenkins' garden —and long after Mr. Jenkins himself had been stowed in a fine mahogany box of his own — they remembered the day when Mr. Jenkins had invited them to listen to the great Caruso on the Victrola, a marvellous machine that had come all the way to Fox Cove from remote and fantastical New York.

*****

*MICHAEL FINN was born and raised in Grand Falls. He has lived in St. John's; Burgeo; Kyoto, Japan; and in St. Bernard's-Jacques Fontaine.*

# Miss Fyfe

## By Michael Nolan

Bertha Beryl Ling-Ling Goobie was left one night in 1937 on the step of St. Jude's Church, pinned down by her name. The priest who tripped over her in the morning thought finding the mother would be easy: Little Heart's Disease (after Confederation, Happy Harbour) was a small place. Yet no woman seemed lighter by the weight of a child; no Goobie confessed or boasted of being father — and the closest Goobie was, in any case, two communities distant and Anglican; no stranger had been seen; no rumour was heard.

Soon it all seemed like a devilish practical joke and after Father O'Brien had delivered more than one searching homily about the sanctity of truth and the scorching of hell, he was about to contact the archbishop and Belvedere Orphanage. Then a couple, newcomers, asked to take home the child. Over a cup of tea in the priest's front room, the child was exchanged, both sides equally relieved by the bargain. The body was to be with the Presbyterian Fyfes; the soul, however, would be Catholic.

The Fyfes were older and childless, retired from the civil service from somewhere in Ontario. (The wife had connections in Newfoundland.) They had set up a convenience store acquired from a local crushed by the Depression. Business was good, but the Fyfes were not loved like Mr. O'Leary had been; they were always CFA's, never friendly enough, and never gave the store credit customers were used to.

The girl, Bertha Beryl Ling-Ling still, but Goobie-Fyfe now, was loved with all the force that frustrated parenthood could bring. The couple wanted their child to be safe. So the girl stayed indoors and picked at books, growing soft and fat, while those who might have been her friends fell down hills and pelted the gulls and each other. When she got to school, the single room for grades 1 to 5, she sat in her desk like a stone, the rest of the room chatting and laughing. Her first day, the three other new students circled round her and mocked the neatness of her dress and the shininess of her shoes. She fled home crying.

When the classmates learned her full name, which the teacher, green from school herself, thought cute and mentioned, there was no relief for Bertha Beryl Ling-Ling Goobie-Fyfe. The girl, already an alien, became an exile. The Marys and Bridies and Dermots and Cyrils, who only had a handful of surnames between them, laughed at her nominal weirdness. They slurped imaginary cups of tea before her face, with their pinkies stuck up, and jeered at her hyphenated state — Dermot O'Leary's mother taught him the style. They swelled out their scrawny bellies, rolling around the schoolyard with "Big Fat Bertha" on their tongues. They screwed up their eyes and chanted "Ring-Ring," buzzing like a chorus of phones. If they could have figured out how to scorn Beryl, they would have done that, too.

The girl cried to her mother, but the woman couldn't help. "Just ignore them" is easily said but is never useful. "Oh, why, did you make me keep these stupid names?" wailed the little one. "Oh, dear girl," hugged the mother, who braved the coldness of customers everyday, "names are not important. Make them see who you are inside. They'll learn how smart and nice you are. How can they not love you like I do?" The girl stared at her mother in astonishment, then bawled louder and roared to her room.

Yet she tried to be pleasant. She shared her dolls, but they got stolen; she helped with math, but just gained more names. She tried to be funny, but no one laughed.

Once or twice she showed up at class, saying that she'd changed her name, but no one called her Margaret or Betty. Schoolyard-wide incantations of her own long name broke her hopes. When one morning, a little mad, she declared herself Shannigetti — English name April Flower — the last of the Beothuks, one of the Brendans tried to scalp her. She tried no more self-christenings.

Life was dullness at home and terror at school, until she was 12, when she went to Confirmation. St. Jude's was packed, not only with those about to be confirmed from freshly constituted Happy Harbour and the surrounding towns and their families, but everybody else: the bishop was to preside. Everyone was soap-smells and ironing-stiff, but there was a sunniness to the day. There were handshakes outside the church and smiles within. Even Bertha, lined in the front pew with the girls, felt that maybe she'd have a chance now: she'd be reborn after Confirmation as Theresa. Yet as the bishop entered, all colour and choirboys, Mary O'Brien whispered, "Look Missus Fancy-Drawers, don't think this will make you one of us."

Then there was a rending of a white confirmation dress and a wail of damnation that chilled the very incense in the air. The church boomed. The people quaked. Bertha scrambled over two Marys and onto the altar. She bumped "Uncle" Cecil O'Leary off the organ and pounded away, her unloosed bun shaking hair about her ears. Screams and wails piped against the vault and against the heart. Then Bertha flung back the stool, faced the pews and the dumb-faced crowd, gave a shriek, then rushed to an alcove and launched a statue. The Virgin ascended partly to Heaven and then curved to Earth, a shattering of dusty plaster across the nave.

Now the faithful themselves convulsed, smacked at once across the face. There was a chorus of cry, but Bertha dashed before they could: up the stairs and inside a door. Banging and smashing and dragging roared down the stairs. Heads turned to the bishop; heads against the Fyfes. There was an exit to the door, like the buzz of wasps, then an exhale of anger outside. A red-faced mob swarmed around the Fyfes, all spiteful indignation. "This is all your mainland ways," one hissed. "Go back where you came from," spat another. "That Ling-Ling was always cracked," accused a girl.

Then the jostling started, shirt fronts and dress pleats rustling loud. The bishop, human and gaudy, made peeps of peace, but no one listened. Someone grabbed Mr. Fyfe by the collar. A howl let loose. Then, with a sudden heave, the mob was parted. A tall man stood before the Fyfes. He held a steady eye upon the crowd, full upon its leaders. The protests stilled. Then he spoke: "No one has cause to do these people harm. They've done no wrong. Give us room and we'll clear this up."

An O'Leary dared one look, but slunk away. Newfoundland Ranger Murphy, not yet issued an RCMP uniform, and in his Sunday best, turned to the couple behind him.

"Are you the mother? Mrs. Fyse?" he asked.

"Fyfe."

"Sorry. What's your daughter's name?"

"Bertha."

"I'll go and talk with her. It'll be fine."

He entered the church. His body cut the fine sunlit smoke.

He knocked gently on the upstairs door. "Miss Fyfe? It's Constable Murphy. I'm here to help. Would you let me in, Miss Fyfe?"

A heart leapt inside. Then the door swung open.

*****

MICHAEL NOLAN *was born and educated in St. John's. He teaches English at Memorial University. He enjoys acting and playing hockey. He won one of the 2010 Arts & Letters Awards for short story.*

# The Goat

### By Joshua Goudie

Their house fell apart a little more every day. Paint flaked and the occasional piece of siding fell. And none of us ever heard or got a look at any of them. In truth, the only sign that anyone actually lived there was the backlit tarpaulin that hung from the lower lip of their second-floor veranda. It was red and they kept the light on behind there 24/7.

At night the flickering streetlights were like floating embers compared to the roaring blaze beneath that house. It was as if the taut, bloodshot plastic was the evening's cell for the captured morning light. As boys, when we walked by at night we always expected something behind there to shake or grumble, but not even the wind seemed able to disturb it. Whatever was behind there was hidden, and hidden with reason. It's strange how the quietest homes can sometimes be the biggest disturbances.

Sam and I lived at opposite ends of the street just off Military Road. He still had the full family unit, while I was a child of divorce. At least that's what Mom says. I've never met my dad or seen a wedding photo so it could just be that he ran out on her before anyone had a ring over their finger. We probably would have been the odd family on the block had it not been for the ones with the tarpaulin. God bless them in that way.

Sam and I used to play together but I haven't seen him in years. Not since both our childhoods were gulped away in one awful set of nights.

Sam started acting strange a few weeks before we were supposed to start school. At first it was little things, like we stopped going over to his house to play. But then things started getting bigger. Like, even once I was called in for supper, sometimes I'd see him out the window, just walking up and down the street. It was like he didn't want anyone, himself included, to be inside his house. I know why now, but I didn't then.

We used to play in the woods behind my house. We'd throw a ball around or play capture the flag or just have a bit of fun taking out our birds and flooding ants nests. It was all innocent. We were only six, sure.

But then Sam started getting really out of sorts. Like something else was always inside his mind. He wasn't talking as much and he was jumpier than usual. He even got sent home on the first day of school for beating the snot out of some other kid for no reason at all.

It was like he was in constant pain. And he was.

One day when we were in the woods, I watched him start to cry from out of nowhere, then he pulled down his pants and let loose an awful spray of blood. "Please don't tell," he asked, with pants still around his ankles. Thin red streams were still tracing their way down his skinny white legs like raindrops on a window.

After that he stopped coming out altogether. I'd still see him at school, though he wasn't much to talk to anymore.

One night I woke up from a bad dream and went to my window to get a bit of air, when I saw him. It must have been after two, but there he was, standing in front of that house, leaning on their fence and staring, like that red tarp and whatever was behind it didn't scare him anymore.

A few nights later I was watching TV when I saw the lights outside the window; a non-stop cycle of blue and red. They were down past the house with the burning red wall, but beyond that, I couldn't tell whose house they were parked in front of. But when Sam didn't show up to school the next day, I had a good idea.

He didn't show up to school for the rest of the week either. I didn't see him again until that Saturday night when he came knocking on my door in new blue jeans and an oversized white T-shirt. When I asked him what was going on he told me that we had something we needed to do. I was sure he knew what I had really been getting at but I thought better of asking twice.

We stopped in front of the house with the flaking paint, overgrown grass and glowing red screen. I watched as Sam kicked in the worn, wire gate and moved, as if on autopilot, towards the tarp.

I don't know why he asked me to come along. He had a purpose and it didn't seem like he needed my help. He didn't even turn around to look at me before grabbing hold of the plastic sheet and pulling with all his might.

The floodlights behind the curtain knocked out our eyes and for a few seconds we were blind.

We had our heads down, rubbing at our eyes with our fists when we both caught sight of why the darn thing never moved. All around our ankles were cinder blocks to hold the tarp taut.

I still can't make any sense of why someone would keep such a thin, emaciated goat locked up like that. From the look of him he couldn't have been much more than a baby, but maybe he was older. You just couldn't tell anymore.

He lay in the dirt, skin clinging to veins, bone and what little muscle he had left. He looked like he was already gone only he swelled up like a balloon with every breath he took. I started to cry. It was his little horns that did it. I don't know why, but he just looked so cute and pathetic all at once and I couldn't take it.

Neither could Sam as it turned out. He bent down, rubbed the poor thing's face with his hand, then got up and went for one of the cinder blocks.

He was as merciful as he could have been. He didn't throw or slam it down or anything. He just let it drop.

And that was all it took.

"No one should have to live with that much pain," he said.

I don't know why people sometimes do the things they do.

The next night the floodlights turned off. The night after that someone threw a flaming beer bottle through their front window and burnt the place to the ground. On the news the fire department said that no one was hurt, but still, I didn't see anyone come out of that house.

We never even knew their names.

*****

*JOSHUA GOUDIE was born in Grand Falls-Windsor, attained a bachelor of fine arts degree from Memorial University and now works as a writer full-time.*

# Stranger in the Shed

## By Samuel Thomas Martin

Les has no idea as he trudges toward his shed that Trish Neary is hiding in there, huddled in her nightdress, the side of her face bloody and her ear bitten off.

All he knows is that he can't fry fish on a cold stove so he needs more wood.

Keeping the fire going is his baby. Ever since Mealy's heart attack in May which he blames himself for. He'd had his cataracts removed a week prior and was letting her do all the work while he convalesced. He figures she overdid it. So he does everything now: cooking, keeping the fire lit.

Earlier he'd run an extension cord from the house to the Christmas lights he leaves up year round in the scraggly pine out front. Mealy asked him to. She'd also asked him to pull some fish out of the freezer and fry it up for supper. So he'd scraped the blue spots off the butter and spooned some into the pan but soon realized the wood stove was icy.

That's why he's on his way to grab some junks of spruce. But that thought zips clear out of his head when he opens the door and sees a blue girl in a nightshirt shivering against the far wall, fear iced in her eyes and the side of her face all bloody.

Mother o' God.

The shed is dark and the girl's quivering lips mutter "please." Les sees the feathers of two of his darts in her one hand, and a third dart in her other shaking fist.

"I'm not gonna hurt ya," he says.

Her face cringes like a beaten mutt and she drops the two-fisted darts and reaches a hand to her mangled ear.

"Who did this to you?"

She looks past Les and whispers, "Ben."

He thinks a moment. Then it clicks: "You're Trish Neary. Green door down the road? All those wind chimes."

She nods. Looks out the door. Back at him. He can see her hands cradling her belly. "It's not his," she spits blood. "And he found out!"

Les takes a step toward her and she cowers. "Whoa," he soothes. "You're safe here."

"He's tracking me! He'll find me. He always finds me."

Les has heard of Ben Neary from up the road. Crack shot at 300 yards. Boasted to the boys at the Township that he once tracked a moose three days in pouring rain and killed it with a hunting knife. Slit its throat. Les has also seen the guy's busted knuckles and smelled rum on his breath more than once before the young lad got in his salting truck and drove out of the municipal yard.

Arsehole, he'd thought, but this—

Trish is staring ball-eyed at the open door.

"We'll get you inside. Okay? Lock the door. Call the cops."

He grabs a quick armload of wood and ushers Trish quickly to the house, calling for Mealy. Her La-Z-Boy squeaks as she drops the footrest.

"You got the wood?" She calls from the other room.

"Mealy! Come here!"

She grumbles, clicks her walker and chokes when she comes around the corner and sees Trish Neary standing in a muddy nightdress and Les' jackshirt, the side of her head blood-smeared: stained hands shaking and touching her ear gingerly.

Les: "Can you clean her up while I phone the RNC?"

"What happened to you, girl?"

"She's stunned."

"I see that. Go on, get that fire lit."

Soon the kindling is crackling. Mealy has her kit out on the counter and is perched on her walker, dabbing at Trish's mangled ear with iodine — the girl letting out whimpers.

Les: "You give her any Tylenol?"

"You called the cops yet?"

"I was just getting this started."

"Fire never should've been put out."

"You give her pills?"

"I'll look after her. You give them a ring. And cook up that fish after. She needs something in her belly."

Les scrapes the cast iron pan over the heat. Then he reaches for the phone. He hears Trish scream and Mealy coddle and the phone ring on the other end. Three tones, a click, a woman's voice.

He tells her a girl's got her ear bitten off. But he doesn't hear how the woman responds because he's looking at Mealy placing both her hands over Trish's fingers cupping the young girl's belly. "Sir?" He hears from the other end. "Yeah, no, I think she's pregnant," he whispers.

"What house are you?" The voice crackles.

Les looks down and draws a blank: keyboard keys clacking on the other end.

"Sir?"

"Just comin' into Fawkes Cove. On the left. There's a mangy Christmas tree in the yard. Lights are on."

"And the woman with the bitten-off ear: she's okay?"

"Yeah," he says, inhaling, looking at Trish leaning against the sink. Crying. Mealy wiping dried blood from the girl's forehead and face. He hears the woman's voice crackle and he almost shouts into the receiver: "Just tell your boys to get down here! The prick that did it is still loose."

"Sir—"

Click. He recalls how quickly the ambulance got to the house when Mealy collapsed on the floor in May. Fifteen minutes to make a 30-minute drive from St. John's. His wife's body crumpled on the linoleum where she's standing shakily now, doctoring.

He can't fathom what would drive a man to bite a girl's ear off and her pregnant.

He sees the lights on the tree through the window above the chipped enamel sink. Mealy's telling Trish to watch the lights as she continues cleaning the girl's bloodied face.

Les flips the fish, smells the scorched butter browning. Sees the wash of red, blue and green through the window. White gauze around Trish's head, her skin purpling with bruises in the rising heat. The smell of fried fish. Peroxide. Les gets the girl some of Mealy's clothes from the bedroom and holds them under his arm on the way back to warm them. Then he hands over the purple slacks and flowery top, turns his back and serves up the pan-fried trout as Trish changes out of her bloodied nightgown.

He doesn't know why but he lights a candle. Sets it on the table. The cheap wax sputters and the wick smokes and curls.

Trish is in his chair but he doesn't say anything. He fiddles with his fork as Amelia prays and Trish looks across the table at him, fire in her eyes — staring out from under white gauze wrapped around her head. "Thank you," she mouths through broken lips. And he sees it now, clear as a scar on an open palm. Candlelight pools on the softwood table. Light wobbles and washes over dark-veined wood, dinted and heat-marked. Gouged. Flickering glow. He sees it clearer now, like since they carved the cataracts from his eyes. Crackle from the stove. Clink of forks on plates. Flakes of fish melting in their mouths. Taste of summer gone, yet to come. That poor girl's battered face, her cracked lip — he sees it there. Silence pregnant and full of breathing. Waiting for tires on gravel. Hoping to hear sirens soon.

*****

*SAMUEL THOMAS MARTIN is the author of* This Ramshackle Tabernacle *(Breakwater 2010), which was shortlisted for the 2010 BMO Winterset Award. His new novel,* A Blessed Snarl, *was published by Breakwater Books in 2012.*

# Written in Bone

## By Michael Collins

The old man couldn't tell what it was. It looked like pale fabric. It looked like whalebone. Like snow. Like nothing. He didn't trust his eyes much anymore. His vision was starting to fail, but he was old enough to know you can't trust your eyes worth a damn regardless of their condition.

He approached. It refused to coalesce into meaning, like a pale hole in reality. It was only as he came closer that he realized some part of his brain had instantly recognized it and quarantined that knowledge.

It was a drowned man. Short brown hair, spiky with salt. Long limbs, bloodless, with black hair in patterns like scrimshaw in an unknown language, runes telling a story if they could be read. He was naked. The old man's eyes flitted across and then away, the quick movements of curiosity and shame when they dance together.

How did the drowned man come to be here? What was his name? Where did he come from? The old man looked for some artifact, some vestige to answer these questions. There was nothing.

Not knowing what to do, he walked on, climbed the hill back to his cabin. He walked this beach for 15 years, since he'd been released, since he'd retreated. He'd never seen the like of this before.

It was three days before Margaret's visit.

He listened to CBC Radio, paid attention to the news. It was always full of RCMP looking for tourists swept to sea or boaters fallen overboard. He heard nothing. Protesters objecting to an office building planned for downtown St. John's. Brigus holding its annual Blueberry Festival. Some Inquiry making its final report. Some other Inquiry starting.

He put the kettle on and thought about the drowned man. He should report it. Him. But what sense was that? It'd only bring the Mounties out. They came by once a week already. To make sure he was Okay, they said in broad prairie accents. They were from away. He told them he was participating in a long Newfoundland tradition of old men living alone until they aren't living anymore. He knew they made these visits because their computers indicated he had a criminal record. "Low risk to re-offend," he quipped once. A blond officer from Lloydminster squinted at him like the words weren't even English.

The drowned man. The kettle had been screaming for God knows how long.

As he poured the boiling water, images of whale corpses emerged from his mind, memories from the station at Rose-au-Rue, memories twisted and corrupted from decades spent unremembered. The long strips of blubber coming clean off the body, the smell of rendering fat. The pale ocean flesh. Then the war came, came up from deeper, bodies mangled, twisted, limbs gone, faces gone, boys choking on foreign mud in foreign fields. His hands in the water. His hands around someone's neck. He set the kettle down. His arms felt too weak for the task. He inhaled steam from the half-full teapot, tried to come back to the present.

He should report the body. A family might be looking for their lost loved one. But what good would it be? He'd lost people — he'd lost everyone but Margaret. Having a body did not lessen a loss. You can focus on the absence of a body, but having a body makes no difference. The person is still gone. So he reasoned.

So the old man filled a bucket with soapy water and prepared to scrub the floors. Margaret would be here in three days.

The half-prepared tea went untouched.

He went back the next morning. He awoke ready to call it a dream. As he aged his dreams became untidy, unruly, began to merge with the material of waking life. He'd remember dreamed things as if real, and real things as if dreamed. A drowned man, unmissed, skin like whalebone, limbs like scrimshaw — surely that was a dream.

But the drowned man was still there, untouched by flies or crows or other carrion-eaters. The old man gently ran his finger along the drowned man's calf. It was smooth, cool, white. He forced himself to look at the body, the double-bowed clavicle, the small nipples, the belly button that showed he was of woman born. The open hands, the delicate testicles. The eyes, closed, closed.

The old man sat there until the sun was down. What thoughts came to him, he couldn't say. Weak with hunger and with thirst, he climbed back to his cabin. His face was wet. Margaret was coming in two days. She couldn't see him like this.

The day before Margaret's visit. He forces himself to make a breakfast but he's in such a hurry the caplin are almost raw and the tea is barely steeped. He scrambles down to the beach.

But the drowned man is gone.

The old man stands in the hollow. His hands by his side. The secret of human life. A loss. "Wait," he says. The steady inhale and exhale of the waves. "Wait."

Margaret pulls onto the shoulder of the highway. This is the closest a car can come.

She visits once a month. It'd be even less, but Lem hates to go into town. Margaret brings him supplies. He doesn't know she's the one who has the RCMP come by regularly.

She gathers bulging Sobeys bags from the trunk and begins the trek to his cabin. She's been told how brave she is, and how foolish. Margaret suspects she is neither.

Lem used to keep a tidy place, but he's become absent-minded lately, prone to leaving tasks half-done. Margaret worries he'll leave something on the stove someday and burn the place down.

He meets her at the door as if no time has passed. They embrace. Margaret allows it. Lem releases her and she goes about putting supplies away. With silent dismay she notes mice droppings in the cupboard. Little dots, Morse code bespeaking ruin.

He is no talker, but Margaret senses he wants to speak. She won't ask him directly, though. "So, how's the weather?" she says breezily as she stacks tins of beans.

"There was something down on the beach," Lem begins. "Something ..."

Margaret keeps a steady rhythm to her work, a neutral tone to her voice. "Yes, dear?"

"It was," he begins.

"Yes?"

"It was...." His words come so slow. She stops, looks at him. He is so old. The air and time between them. "It was nothing." His face shuts. He is dead to the living when like this; nothing can recall him.

Margaret sighs, turns. This again. Her gaze drifts to the few yellowed newspaper clippings on the wall, 30 years old now. They tell of the man her husband drowned, of psychiatric assessment, trial, sentencing. He never, never looks at them, but when Margaret tries to take them down he stops her with a sharp shout. He waits for her hand to come away from the stories and then, only then, his gaze drifts out the little window to the cold ocean beyond them all, as if he expects to see something.

*****

*MICHAEL COLLINS is a writer from Placentia. He holds degrees in English from Memorial University and the University of Western Ontario. He studied poetry in Ireland and is currently pursuing a PhD. He was the 2nd-place winner of 2010's Cuffer Prize, and he has published short fiction in a variety of places.*

# Burning

## By Heidi Mitchell

"You get back here, I'm tellin' you, if you don't get back in this house this minute, I swear to God, you don't come back at all."

I left anyway, swearing under my breath, I didn't need her, nor nobody else. She never even knew who I was anyway.

So I left, I let the screen door slam on my way out, and walked down my driveway with my knapsack slung over one shoulder. I didn't turn around once. I could hear her smashing glass in the house and screaming at me to come back for God's sake and that I was gonna get myself killed if I wasn't careful. I didn't much care, to be honest, either way, dead or alive, whatever.

I rounded one of the gateposts that used to have heavy iron gates on them to keep out the roaming cows and sheep that would be put to pasture up the road in the fields for the summer months, and just kept walking.

My plan was to walk to town, which wasn't really that much of a walk, stay there for a bit and then get to Port aux Basques, somehow; probably thumb my way there. But I was tough, I had all I needed in my knapsack. I could make it, no problem sure. I got halfway around the lake when my uncle pulled up beside me.

"You got to go back," he yelled at me over the idling motor of his '89 Chev.

"I don't got to go nowhere," I yelled back at him.

"Your mudder's gone right mad, she is. You got to go back, I'm tellin' you. You got to. Please, just see to her?"

"She's always right mad, always has been, always will be. I brought Lucy to Nan's to stay there. I'm not takin' care of Mom anymore."

"Well, I don't know what to do with her, she's smashin' up the house. You're the only one who can calm her down. Please, just get in the truck."

"No."

"George Edward Parsons, get in this truck right now."

"No, I'm not goin' back there no more."

So I kept walking, and he kept driving along beside me, his flicker on the entire time, flashing red. There was no way in H-E-double two sticks that I was goin' back. Lucy was safe at Nan's. I didn't want another beatin'. The house was in shambles now, anyways. Nothin' to go back for.

He pulled his truck in ahead of me, grabbed me by the scruff of the neck and shoved me into his truck.

"If you wants to be treated like a man, then bloody well act like one. Now, you'll see to your mother, and you'll stay there with her and you'll take care of her like a reasonable man would. If I hears tell of you leavin' her again, I'll tan your hide so fast you won't know what's comin' to ya. She's sick sure, you knows that, and can't be left alone."

We didn't talk the entire ride home. I just sat there, thinking. Well, there goes school, there goes having my own life, there goes everything.

When we got home the barn was on fire, half the cove just stood there, watching it burn. I shoved past them all, walked slowly up over the steps and opened the screen door.

"Momma!" I called.

"You! What do you think you're doin' 'ere?"

"I came back, Momma. I couldn't leave you." As those words left my mouth, my heart sank. Here was not where I wanted to be. I didn't want to be here, home.

Smoke was beginning to fill the room. "Momma, come outside, let's go for a walk, just us. We'll go to Nan's, have some tea. Come on, Momma, please?"

I thought I had calmed her down a bit. She had stopped throwing things.

"You knows bloody well I don't want to go there. All they wants to do is take me to the mental. I'm not mental, I don't belong there. No sir, I'm not going nowhere. You just wants to get me out of this house so that they can take me away. That's all you wants!" she screamed at me, her eyes burning with hatred toward me, her son, her child.

"No, Momma, I don't want them to take you away and they're not gonna take you away. I'll keep you safe, Momma, I promise I will. Please, let's just go outside and look at the flowers. They're all a-bloom out back. Come on, Momma, let's just go out back and sit in the sun for awhile. It's too nice a day to be inside." I reached for her hand, she took it. I squeezed her hand tight in mine, and smiled at her the best I could.

We walked outside and sat down behind our house, just the two of us, between two burning buildings. The fires kept burning, and eventually all the people left and went home out of it. After darkness had fallen, Momma said to me, "I'm awfully sleepy, baby."

So I let her rest her head on my lap and she curled up and slept soundly. I couldn't sleep. There was no barn no more, there soon wouldn't be a house, and they'd take her away, and it was my fault — no one else's, just mine. And knowing this I sobbed softly until it became uncontrollable, and I shook with all of my being, gasping and crying and shaking and sobbing, waterfalls on my face.

Momma woke up.

She sat up. "It's okay baby, I know you didn't wanna stay. It's all right now, stop your cryin' now." She took off her sweater and put it around my shoulders and hugged me tight into her. "There, there, baby, everything's all right."

In that moment she was my momma again, not the person who didn't even know who I was half the time. She was just my momma again and I was her baby, just liked it used to be before Lucy came along.

After I stopped crying we laid on the grass, with Momma's sweater spread over our arms, cuddled together, looking up, past the smoke, at the stars, laughing about times we could remember. I dunno when, but eventually we fell asleep.

The next morning, I woke first and just watched her sleeping.

When Momma woke up, she was startled and hauled her sweater back to her and moved away from me.

"Who are you?" she yelled.

*****

*HEIDI MITCHELL lives in Portugal Cove-St. Philip's. She is an eager writer, with a stockpile of half-finished short stories. She is also a photographer.*

# The Rising

## By Chantelle Sears

"It's coming, Missus," he stated as he joined us at the table.

Mother frowned. "What?"

"Remember that thing I showed you?"

"Oh, that. Already? How do you know?"

"The gulls."

Had I slipped into a Beckett world? "What are you talking about?"

"I suppose you didn't read the article."

"'The Rising'? I did. But —"

"Now. See, Missus? That's what comes of giving our youngsters a university education. Always a 'but.' Always critical."

"Dad!" The man could exasperate a sea-sponge. "I'm just saying: if you pay attention to every half-baked, doomsday theory offered by all the Chicken Littles out there, you'll drive us all mad."

Mother attempted to squelch his impending derisive snort. "Tell us about the — ahh, Baby. No!"

Little niece had determined that her left ear was the orifice best suited to receive a spoonful of pureed apricots.

As I cleaned the mess, Dad gestured at the window.

Gulls. Not strange to see them soaring in or out the — hang on — these birds, flapping with duck-like frenzy, were heading north and south over the mountains framing the Humber Arm, perpendicular to their usual course.

This same observation had earlier compelled my father to hike up the hill behind our house ...

"Water?" Mother questioned. "You mean the pond?"

"Nope."

Between spoon slurps and grilled-cheese sandwich dips of tomato-parmesan soup, Dad elaborated.

"Water everywhere. Far as the eye can see. Just a foot below the crest. And like the brine."

"But ... how is that possible?"

"Don't know. But it's coming for us, too."

It wasn't possible. And with the transmission line and watersheds in back, we would have been affected by now. Nevertheless, I would play along.

"Then why didn't it happen to us first? We have the Atlantic feed, if some monstrous tidal event occurs."

"Maybe it's not coming from the ocean."

"Then where? Let me guess — all the mining, and drilling for oil — we've sprung a leak."

Dad slammed his fist on the table; I had gone too far. "You won't be so bloody glib by this afternoon!" he roared.

I turned to console a startled, teary Baby.

"Don't ignore me, you—"

"Shouldn't we be evacuating?" Mother intervened.

He sighed. "There's nowhere to go. Judging by the gulls, the whole valley is surrounded."

"Then what do we do?"

I bit my tongue. Probably not wise to suggest we build a raft.

"Wait." He sighed again. "Go about your business."

Jolted by his resignation, I ventured a surreptitious glance at him. What was this? My father, man of a million contingency plans, doing the wait-'n'-see waltz? He had long been obsessed with predictions of world-changing events; however, he had never been so convicted, yet ... ambivalent ...

I was troubled. So, dishes washed, Baby napping in her playpen, Dad mowing the lawn, I decided to take a quick jaunt in back, myself — after a quick Internet search for news of peculiar global flooding. Mother had a different idea: finish the Coleman wedding order. Just in case.

Just in case?

"Mother, you don't actually think ..."

"Of course not. We've rejected The Church; that sign interpretation stuff is rubbish." They kept insisting that.

"So there's nothing to it?"

"Mmm ... Check the radio for news."

I did.

Preset 1: Static ...

Preset 2: Dead air...

Okay; happened occasionally.

Preset 3: "..."

I punched the power button. Wasn't torturing myself with "Chicken 'n Biscuits" and whatever other excuse-for-a-song aired before the next newscast.

For the next hour, Mother candied and I wrapped the sweets we had made before lunch. Usually, the rhythmic snip-wrap-twist of packaging our candy would lull me into a quasi-hypnotic daze; not today.

Logic told me "The Rising" was a gimmick. It was simply not possible for the earth to undergo a rapid, global rise in water levels without a Noahesque rainstorm. And that took days. Still, with a multitude of prophets and prophesies through the millennia, eventually, someone had to be right about something.

Snip-wrap-twist ... Snip-wrap-twist ...

"Ugh!" Mother exploded. "Third batch. It's not setting." She tipped a mold; sticky caramel dripped out.

Dad entered the kitchen, dabbing sweat from his face. "Might need to adjust your thermometer. Look out."

We stood at the window for 15 minutes, transfixed, as the baywater, which had swollen to kiss the edge of the freshly mowed lawn, crept the remaining distance to our house. Then climbing: past planters, foundation, basement windows — the basement! I rushed to the stairwell. Empty. Reached the icy, concrete floor. Bone dry.

Back upstairs, I stood with my parents on the patio. The water seemed to be at a standstill at the top stair-tread.

Dad pointed. "Dolphins." Dozens of them. Two, as if sensing our attention, separated from the others, breaching and diving until they were within our reach. Dad stretched; stroked a glistening snout. "Soft ..." he breathed, and plunged without warning into the rippling pool.

"Dad!" I could only gasp.

"Come in, Missus."

Mother seemed doubtful. "I dunno..."

"Mother, you can't." This was crazy.

She ignored me. "Is it cold?"

"Not really."

"Hang on." She spun around and stepped indoors.

"Dad ... This is insane!"

"Insanity is all in your mind. Remember that."

Mother reappeared, donning a windbreaker. I grabbed her arm.

"Mom. *Stop* ..." Pleading, now.

She shoved me back and then leapt, landing next to my father in the water, jacket parachuting behind her. They began to frolic with the dolphins, laughing and splashing each other.

"Why are you *doing* this?" My throat was raw.

"We're going to swim!" Mother's giggle became a shrill squeal.

"Swim with the *FISH-ies!*"

Dad chimed in as they began to float away from the patio.

"Swim with the *FISH-ies!*"

Frantically, heart racing, I tried again. "What about Baby?"

"Baby's fine," Mother called. "Give her formula if she cries."

They were drifting eastward toward Corner Brook, now, gaining speed. Though I could no longer discern their faces, Mother's final holler carried clearly across the liquid expanse. "And don't forget to lock the door behind you!"

In seconds, they rounded the point, out of sight.

I choked back a sob and stumbled into the house. Baby was crying. She grinned as I passed her a bottle of milk. "Bah." She lay back, sucking noisily; there was dried apricot in her hair.

I wandered back out to the patio. The door swung shut. Remembering, I opened it, turned the lock, and latched it gently.

More people were bobbing in the bay. Their shrieks echoed off the far hills.

"Swim with the *FISH-ies!*"

A pink sloop slowed near Curling's now-submerged oil tanks.

It was getting breezy; the water slapped softly against the patio edge, higher, beckoning. I stepped forward. *No!*

Dizzy, slightly nauseated, I clutched the railing. I was thirsty; shivering, I groped for the door ... twisted the knob. Right. Locked.

I collapsed against the house, sliding down to sit on the deck, hugging my knees to my chest.

Deep in my soul, it erupted: a haunting loon-call-wolf-howl fusion that ripped through my heart and lungs.

I gulped.

*This is not happening.*

*Swim with the FISH-ies!*

*All in your mind.*

Blinked.

The pink sloop was dropping anchor.

*Swim with the FISH-ies!*

The keening bubble clawed at my throat.

I closed my eyes and let it rise.

*****

*CHANTELLE SEARS lives in Corner Brook.*

# Caribou

## By Laura O'Brien

John held the wrinkled black and white picture up to the horizon and scanned the landscape until he could match the rock formation and the slope of the hill to the exact spot it had been taken.

It had taken him a while to find the location. The defining details in the barrens are subtle and the fog had been thick in the early morning and was only now beginning to burn off. When the scene suddenly locked into place John's breath momentarily halted. It was a strange optical illusion, as if the present day was playing on a screen and just behind a tear in that fabric there was a duplicate movie playing. An old silent movie, forever paused in time.

The younger people in the photo had looked just as pleasant for almost 40 years. But he felt the weight of that time on his back and shoulders, unimaginable to the smiling bright-eyed boy leaning back on the grass. Grass is grey in black and white, as young flesh is also grey. The dissipating fog drew back the shade from a grey world before him and he wondered how insignificant his age was to the hard ground before him. Standing on the sparsely covered stone, he felt the greater weight of a geological age sweep his own insecurities aside with an indifferent shrug.

He shivered slightly and looked around. Other than a bench and a battered barrel garbage can, the place remained the same. The unchangeability of a place makes it feel proper for a reunion, he thought.

"There are cars here. If we stop, there might be a way in. I'd not want to cross that bog."

"I don't know what you want that for. There's far better stuff in bottles."

"You stop here, now."

The car eased to a halt on the gravel at the side of the road. She opened the door and stepped out and walked across to where the grass began to grow on the edge of the gravel. "I'm going to ask someone," she called back.

He walked to where she had stood and stared out across the rocks and scrub bushes. There was a smell to this place not quite like any he'd smelled before. He rubbed his arms, stiff from the long drive.

Ellie was talking to a man who was sitting in the back of his station wagon. He was paused mid-motion pulling off rubber boots. John heard the man laugh. "No, not a one."

"Oh," she said. She sounded disappointed.

"Hello," John said and nodded his head to the man in the car. The man squinted up and winked. "So no bakeapples?"

"Last year, yes. Tons. This year, nothing."

Ellie bobbed up and turned quickly, the smile blooming on her face, "Then we'll just go have our lunch over there and maybe do something else." She ran on ahead with the bucket over the barrens and John watched her white floral dress cut out of the blue horizon and thought at how quickly she could go from disappointment to exuberance.

He remembered the way she moved, more than what they had said. The slight bounce as she turned, the smile, images he could project over the cold landscape revealing itself to him through the burgeoning light. I will let this lens restore the colour to this world, he thought and closed his eyes.

She'd made him get snacks, strawberry Dixie Cups and Keep Kool Root Beer. He'd found a shack that sold french fries on paper plates and brought those back as well. She was delighted.

"Hold still. Can you stop for a one bloody second and let me take a picture!" he called out trying in vain to capture her through the viewfinder.

"All right, all right." She skipped back towards him, "If you'll be in it with me. But that'll mean you'll have to actually smile for a second," Ellie teased as she poked his side and grabbed the camera from his grasp.

She glanced back in the direction where the man had been but he was nowhere to be found. "Hmmm ... I know ..." Ellie put the camera on a low chunk of granite jutting up from the ground. "Hurry!" She grabbed his hand, "We've only got 15 seconds."

In a scramble they ran hand in hand just a few short metres before tumbling down side by side on the ground. John could see only her face through the sunshine and smiled, just as the camera gave a quick flash.

He tilted his head up to search out the sun with his eyes closed. The light that cannot be seen can sometimes be felt. But not in this lonely place, he thought. He wondered if any real warmth ever penetrated the ground. Certainly not enough to crack these stones, he thought.

As he turned to walk back to where he'd parked, the vivid image of a young Ellie standing on the highest stone with her arms stretched out and overjoyed caused him to stop and search out that location. She had been so excited to see the herd in the distance and wanted so badly to run over to where they meandered so quietly. "This is lucky," he'd said at the time, "We must be here on just the right day. I guess they pass through here."

She shook her head but did not look away. "I don't want a picture of this," she whispered.

He sat on the stone and pressed the heel of his hand to his eye. There were so many moments thereafter, but he could sense very sharply the moments that made them who they truly were to one another. He felt the loss immobilize him and he stared after the ghost of the caribou in the distance.

*****

*LAURA O'BRIEN is a "Grace Baby" born in St. John's. Her formative years in relation to writing were spent at Memorial University where she first fell in love with English literature. Laura holds an English degree from MUN as well as a diploma in visual communications from P.E.I. She attributes most of her writing and creative point of view to her time spent in conversation with others. This story is the result of such time and of recent driving trips around the island.*

# Salve Regina

## By Ellen Alcock

Regina awoke at the Women's Shelter feeling hungry and angry. She had to get out before the social worker tracked her down again for one of those earnest conversations about moving into a more permanent housing arrangement. "No goddamn way," swore Regina to every social worker she'd ever met. "There's no way that I'm gonna move into one of them homes out in the friggin' boonies — in Kelligrews, no less!"

Regina loved downtown; even when she was young, she loved Water Street. After school, she'd race down Pilot's Hill to see what was on the go and maybe get some chips. The London, Ayre's, and Bowring's, beautiful stores that firmly anchored the local retail trade, offered all manner of things gorgeous. And when Freddy was still alive, she had lots of those gorgeous things — dresses, shoes, hats, purses. Back then, she could turn heads — "Best lookin' wife around," boasted Freddy. That was before she had to go to work at the hotel — long before she'd ever seen a VLT.

Even the smell of the fumes from the St. John's buses gave Regina a comforting feeling. Sometimes she and her older brother Gary would get on the bus and keep getting transfers until some bus driver caught onto their game and kicked them off downtown, much to their delight. Those were faraway days, long before Gary got the bright idea at 16 to go to Toronto in 1966. One cold March morning, he sprinted down from the top flat and headed out the front door all cocky with Brylcreem in his hair and a smoke dangling from his gob. "I'll send you some money as soon I get a job, Mudder," and with a wink and a nod, and a peck on his mother's cheek, he was gone.

Mrs. Barrington barred the wooden storm door with a resigned thump and went back to making bread, predicting, "That's the last we'll see of him." And she was right. Less than six months later the cops told her that someone had done up Gary in an alley off Yonge Street. A Mrs. Gosse from Torbay, who lived in Toronto, had him buried and Agnes Barrington sent her a cheque every month till the burial was paid off. Regina couldn't even remember now where Gary was buried.

Heading out into the June sunshine in her bulky down-filled jacket, Regina needed a drink — something the loonie in her pocket wasn't gonna get her. At Rawlin's Cross, she tossed her recyclable supermarket bag on a green wooden bench next to that stupid plaque celebrating the arrival of electricity in St. John's. She had a spook around the base of a concrete garbage container where she managed to find a Cameo butt, friggin' menthol, and a stubby Export 'A'.

She lit the Export 'A' and sucked back a few draws before her fingers started to burn. She had managed to get a few shekels off a couple of mainland tourists moping out from a B&B just before a car came around the corner and the cop gave her a look. She grabbed her bag and headed down Queen's Road; her most recent encounter with the cops landed her in the lockup and was followed by a stint at the Waterford Hospital. She vowed never to repeat that ordeal at the Waterford with a bunch of so-called psychologists quizzing her on expectations and quality of life. Regina played along with them and managed to get back on the street in less than two weeks. The world was full of do-gooders — best to avoid them.

By the time she got down to Water Street, Regina had hit up a few cronies and now needed only a toonie to get a flask. If she could scare up a couple of pills to go with that, she'd be right as rain by the afternoon.

Not waiting for the bus, she leaned against the bus stop and smelled the coffee wafting from the new bistro across the street. Pretty quiet there now but there'd be a constant stream of people coming and going by mid-morning. Sometimes the owner, a foreign guy with a pony tail, would give her a coffee and one of his fancy cakes just to get her to move on. She was hungry enough for one of those cakes this morning and she was gonna have one. Regina darted out into the street making a beeline for the front door of the bistro. A young fella in a bread truck piled on the brakes and laid on the horn as he swerved to avoid hitting her. Regina gave him the finger, told him where to go, and continued along the sidewalk muttering something about arseholes being everywhere.

She looked in through the open bistro door. She loved the big black and white floor tiles and the way the cakes were displayed in the glass case. Not good — the owner wasn't there. Chelsea, the girl by the cash, always had that same knot of contempt in her face every time she looked at Regina. The boyish-looking waiter, Mike, was setting up chairs around the little tables by the front window.

Regina marched into the bistro and gawked at the sweets in the case. She figured out which cake she wanted and looking up spotted the fish bowl marked "Tips" on top of the glass case. It already contained coins and bills which were most likely put there by the staff to encourage generous tipping.

In a preachy voice, the waiter said, "Now, now, Regina, those tips aren't for you. You should move along now."

Regina sized him up in his black pants and white apron looking all neat and preppy; he really pissed her off. She grabbed the rim of the fish bowl and ran out to the sidewalk. The loonies and toonies spun noisily around as she swung the bowl over her head and released it into the air screaming, "I don't want your goddamn tips anyway!"

It sounded like a shotgun going off when the bowl hit the front window sending glass flying everywhere. The blood from Mike's arms dripped onto his white apron. Even Regina got a nice gash over her left eye from the flying debris. She tore up the street like a mad woman leaving the two young ones screaming like banshees and slipping on broken glass.

Because Regina was so wiry, she was able to beat it up McBride's Hill and even got as far as Military Road in what seemed like no time. She knew the cops wouldn't be far behind. Maybe this time she had actually overdone it; she was losing her breath and feeling a bit dizzy.

When she fell backwards, her head hit the corner of the concrete steps at the top of Father Walsh's Hill. Lying on the sidewalk, she could see the big white statue of St. John on the arches in front of the Basilica. Sister Bernadette said St. John was holding a baptismal shell; Gary always said it was a bowling ball. Regina smiled as St.

John spun around and around and around — she was sure Gary was right.

\*\*\*\*\*

*A native of St. John's, ELLEN ALCOCK holds BA and MA degrees in English from Memorial University. She enjoys cooking and hiking the East Coast Trail with her husband, Ray.*

# The Visitor

## By Michael Collins

It was upon them before thought. John and Andrew. It was upon them. A piece of the forest gathered itself into the shape of a moose. It separated itself from the trees and was upon them.

It stepped onto the asphalt with thoughtless ease, huge, an affront to "highway," to "car," to "Christmas holiday," to all the rest of human life. The moose was irrefutable.

But this is thinking about the moose, and it was upon them before thought.

"Jesus!" John stood on the brake and cut the wheel. Momentum, the resistance to change built into the universe, lifted a half-full cup of Diet Coke into the air. Watery Diet Coke from a fountain machine in a fast food spot attached to a gas station miles ago. Momentum. Diet Coke sprayed the windshield, brown and thin.

The car heaved itself into stillness, slantaways to the yellow line, its bumper just a foot from the moose. Andrew was an American and had never seen a moose. Barely knew that something like a moose could exist. Andrew saw the way the animal's hair lay over its skin, its muscle. Could see all the little motion of life in its unbelievable body, see it through a sheen of Coca-Cola, diet Coca-Cola, diet Coca-Cola rapidly beading, gathering, moving in channels along unbroken glass. The animal exceeded him.

John was a Newfoundlander. He'd used all the breath in his body when he yelled "Jesus!" He hadn't inhaled since. Snowflakes the same colour as the sky drifted without meaning between the moose and the car, between the moose and the forest. Every muscle in John's body was tense and full of knowledge of the body's mortality.

The moose looked at the two young men. It looked through the snowflakes and through the windshield and through the Diet Coke. It looked at them for an unmeasured moment and then it flicked its ears and finished moving across the highway, its awkward loping gait. It merged with the dark forest that had given it form. The only things to attest it'd ever been were two fresh-formed patterns in two human brains, patterns at the site in the brain's geography where experience turns to memory. There is a name for it: hippocampus. A moose almost killed you. Could have killed you. The smell of flat Diet Coke. It'll be in your hippocampus, waiting to be called forth into mind. Stepping into thought as the moose stepped into the road.

"Jesus." Andrew repeated John's word. But it was not the same as when John said it. John had hurled the word at the moose like a spear. In Andrew's mouth it was not a curse. It was a taking in, not a spitting out.

\*\*\*

There was silence and the empty highroad. John spoke first. "Give me something to wipe this down with. Fuck, it's on my jeans. Ninety-dollar jeans."

"I don't have anything. There's nothing."

"Well give me the Jesus takeout bag. No napkins in that?" John's way of speaking came out.

Andrew looked into the back seat for the takeout bag. "Pull over, there's a car coming behind us."

"Well fuck 'em for a lark, I'm takin' my time. Christ. I hates the sight of a moose. Lookit me hands shake." The car moved to the shoulder of the highway like it was wounded. John put the hazards on.

\*\*\*

The strangeness of another family's house. No. The strangeness of a foreign home in a foreign land. Not the purchased conformity of suburbia. The little differences and the surprising similarities and the way things smell just a little wrong. The impossible-to-dismiss idea that the floors are somehow sticky.

"Moose," Mr. Whalen says with too much enthusiasm, putting a plate before Andrew. "Moose for the mainlander. A delicacy. Bet you don't get no moose down in South Carolina."

The thickness of the muscle tissue. Its undeniable existence. The vein of fat. The suggestion of a tendon. The way the fibres of muscle layer and layer and layer and fold unto themselves, unto and unto and unto, unto. Cutting it into manageable pieces and chewing and swallowing. Not that different from beef. It should be strange, an entirely new flavour.

John had not told his parents about the moose on the highway.

"Whadya think, Mainland?" Mr. Whalen said. "Plenty more if y'likes."

"It's very good, thank you," Andrew says, because he knows something like this is expected of him. That is what is said.

This would be the right time for John to say they'd almost struck a moose on the highway just a few hours ago but John said nothing. He cut his meat and chewed it and swallowed it with a determination, as if consuming the animal was a task he was committed to. Andrew watched the tendons in John's forearm flex and shift as he sawed his knife through the moose, watched the shape of his jaw change as he chewed, the shape of his neck as he swallowed. The quick up-down. The angle of John's shoulders under his shirt as he hunched forward for the next repetition of the action. Bones under skin. Moving. Still. Moving. John felt Andrew's scrutiny and was compelled to speak.

"Dad goes moose hunting every fall," he said, not putting his knife down. A tiny particle of muscle clung to one of its serrations. One of the endless foldings of the moose hanging from steel.

"Got to get me moose, b'y," Mr. Whalen offered, his speech rhythmic. Andrew did not recognize it, if it was a reference or quotation. Mr. Whalen sensed his hesitancy. "A song," he said. "'*Loves to go a-moose hunting, hunting in the fall.*'"

"Oh. Sorry."

The scraping of metal on ceramic.

When everyone finished the meal Mrs. Whalen stood and began

collecting the dirty plates, her steel hair carefully formed and frozen in place with as much spray as it takes to do. Her blouse was rose, her posture beyond criticism.

"You'll be in the bedroom on the left past the bathroom," she announced as she moved from Andrew to John, his plate clattering onto his plate, "across the hall from John's room."

\*\*\*

Andrew is awake. The room, darkness hiding its unfamiliar geography. The clean sheets smooth and cold. John across the hall. Andrew chooses to believe John is awake. John is awake. Will he knock? The minutes stretch.

The dark unchanging. This is the kind of place that shouldn't have Christmas. Christmas is too ordinary. What business has this island with tinsel. He is in a village ("outport") whose name he has somehow forgotten, in a dark room, surrounded by the Atlantic Ocean. Six hundred miles east of Maine.

John is asleep. The memory of the moose parts the deepest folds of his mind, just as the moose parted the trees. Moving through him like a strange visitor, unspoken, irrevocable.

\*\*\*\*\*

*MICHAEL COLLINS is a writer from Placentia. He holds degrees in English from Memorial University and the University of Western Ontario. He studied poetry in Ireland and is currently pursuing a PhD. He was the 2nd-place winner of 2010's Cuffer Prize, and he has published short fiction in a variety of places.*

# Frank Sullivan's Storm

## By Val B. Russell

The wind hammered the bus windows, causing it to heave and sway over the yellow line. It was going to be another irritating day of snow squalls designed by a mean god to distort Frank's sense of distance and proportion while the mickey of rum under the driver's seat would subdue and liquefy everything into a fluid account of what his life could have been.

When Bonnie walked out on him, he was gutted but not surprised. He'd been waiting for it. After Ben died she'd changed and, to be fair, so had he. That baby was everything to her. He never wanted a kid but there was something about little Ben that got inside you, made you want to be a man, his strong unwavering protector. Then it all changed when Ben turned two. He started falling down, his eyes stopped focusing and when he took the first seizure, Frank the strong protector disappeared to be replaced by Frank the drunken cowardly bastard who deserted them both. By the time Ben had his second tumour removed, he'd stopped sleeping at the house, choosing instead to live in a furnished flophouse.

Frank pulled onto the shoulder of the road and turned off the bus engine. He slid his hand under the seat to retrieve his mickey, taking four good swigs; one for each of his failures. He felt the familiar cascading burn of the rum, transcending the lies of his life and filling his chest with a calm superiority that for a while made him believe he no longer gave a shit about life. Somewhere off in the distant past he could see his father passed out and bleeding by the side of the road in Renews, his mother still in her nightdress grabbing his father's arms while 10-year-old Frank took his legs. Into the house they went, dropping him on the floor of the bedroom because neither of them had the strength to lift him as high as the bed.

"What odds," his mother said. "He's probably shit himself anyway and I don't want that filth on the sheets."

In the night his father would come to and sing out for his mother, but she never answered his calls. He was left to lie in this nightly squalor of his own piss and vomit. The next day he'd be gone again and Frank's mother would be on her hands and knees with a bucket and brush, scrubbing the floorboards, cursing both God and the devil for her lot in life. Frank always escaped her by squirreling himself away in the shed where he'd smoke the cigarette butts he'd collected from the old coffee can his Uncle Chris kept by the back door. Even from this distance he could still hear his mother cursing, waging war with the men who had let her down.

His father died the following December and when they found him on his back in front of the Christmas tree he was clutching his chest with one hand while holding a crumpled ten-dollar bill in the other. Frank's mother pried it loose from his fingers before the doctor arrived and stashed it down the front of her dress. She used it to buy a turkey for his wake.

Frank took the last swallow from the mickey, draining the contents to blur memories and the dirty emotions that feasted on them like parasites. He tossed the empty bottle out of the window and started the bus. The kids would be ready for pick-up in 15 minutes and it was going to take him at least 10 to get there. One more late complaint was what that grimy fucker Strickland needed so he could fire his arse. Frank put an angry foot on the gas pedal, wondering if the bus would hit a patch of ice and not caring much if it did.

The bus careened down the main road past the arm and his cousin Jimmy's house, where Frank was sleeping off a bender the day little Ben died. It was stormy then too, the wind howling like a hungry dog on the prowl. By the time he'd sobered up and gotten to the hospital, his son had slipped away surrounded by everyone except his father. When Frank walked into Ben's room his sister-in-law slapped him across the face before walking out while Bonnie lay sobbing across their son's tiny body. Instead of facing it all, he ran out of the hospital and never saw Bonnie again until the funeral. He couldn't explain why but he wasn't able to do it, to help her. He just didn't have it in him.

Frank was starting to sweat and shake again by the time he reached his destination. Turning into the school parking lot he felt relieved; the noisy kids were a welcome and needed distraction from himself. Once the youngsters were loaded on he'd be calm again. The other drivers hated the ruckus kids made, always bawling at them to shut up, but Frank found the din they created a cure for the poison thoughts that crept in through the holes and cracks in his silent purgatory.

The school doors opened, the kids spilling out in small cliques. The boys showing off like peacocks, bellowing and roughhousing in the snow while the girls whispered in a conspiracy of adolescent shyness. Ben could've been one of those boys now if he'd lived. Just as his thoughts threatened to flood Frank's heart with renewed anguish, a group of boisterous 13-year-old boys tramped up the steps making fun of each other, yanking him back to reality.

When the bus was full Frank pulled onto the main road. The traffic coming out of St. John's was heavier than usual and navigating around the other vehicles was taking every bit of Frank's concentration. With the rum in his blood and the fists of wind pummeling the side of the bus it was proving almost impossible to stay in his lane. By the time they reached Ruby Line, only 10 of the 25 kids who were on his route remained. Frank took the corner too tight, nearly colliding with a pickup truck but he soon righted the bus, congratulating himself on his finessing a close call.

The wind continued to rock the bus but it moved along at a good pace and Frank was enjoying the banter in the back, glad it was the weekend and nearly the end of his shift. His black cloud mood was lifting and for a moment he felt like he did before Ben got sick.

Somewhere close to Pitts Memorial Drive the bus skidded on some black ice, sending it hurtling into the intersection, hitting a woman and her baby going southbound in a blue Mazda. Frank tried to control the skid but it was too late when he'd hit the car. As the bus spun Frank was catapulted through the windshield before it rolled over, landing on its side in the middle of the road, broken bits of bloody glass everywhere; the storm still raging around but no longer within Frank Sullivan.

*****

*VAL B. RUSSELL is a poet and novelist living in Newfoundland. Her poetry has twice been nominated for the Pushcart prize as well as appearing in literary journal anthologies such as* Caper Literary, Sibling Rivalry *and* Voxpoetica. *She is currently reviewing books for Her circle magazine while completing a novel.*

# Dinks

### By Ed Turpin

"Game a' dinks?" Stevie sung out from the next yard. Will had his head down on the other side of the fence, kneeling over an anthill with a magnifying glass. He was the Sun God, wreaking havoc on the ant community for no good reason at all. Ants crawled all over his knees, futilely returning fire.

"Sure, b'y!" Will answered, dropping the torture device and leaving the ants to regroup and rebuild before the next attack. He popped to his feet and ran into the house with his shoes on, past his mother's empty stare. He made straight for his room at the end of the hall, and like a baserunner stealing a base, he partially slid under his bed on the hardwood floor to retrieve his shoebox full of dinkies. In the same motion, he collected the box, pushed himself out from under the bed, and tore off towards the sunny day outside. His mother was seated at her usual spot at corner of the kitchen table, smoking cigarettes and gazing out the window.

"See ya, mudder!"

"Where you going?"

"Rockpile!"

"Be good."

"K!"

Stevie was already there, constructing roads in the dirt with his cupped hand and a small piece of wood. Without looking up, he asked, "Got the grader?"

"Sure, y'knows I do."

"Right on. Pitch it."

Will took out the slightly oversized grader and carried it over to

Will and placed it in front of him. "Remember the rules," he reminded Stevie.

"Not stunned, y'know."

Will didn't respond, and went back to his shoebox and poured the dinks on the future site of Willville, Newfoundland. Population: 2. Incorporated 1973. Endless possibilities of roads and schools and houses and hospitals and car accidents.

Will and Stevie called it the Rockpile, but it was really a hump of unused fill behind their houses, perfect for 10-year-old imaginations and dinkies. He looked at the dinkies spread out on the ground. He had a Mustang and a Cadillac and an exaggerated muscle car with oversized tires and a VW Bug and pickups and trailers and taxis and helicopters and police cars and vans and all kinds of vehicles.

He picked out the blue and white 1970 Chevelle SS. The roof was squashed almost flat and the driver's side severely dented inward, the result of carefully placed rock drops to create the simulated wreck. He turned it over to see the Hot Wheels logo on the silver bottom and ran his fingers over it, as if reading Braille. His first act, as it always was when starting a game of dinks, was to kneel in the dirt and create with his hand a stretch of road with a hairpin turn. He carefully placed the mangled 454 on its roof some distance from the curve, and then positioned a tow truck, ambulance, and police car in the area. He put a 1965 Ford Fairlane on the road, as if en route to the scene. Will surveyed the scene for a moment, adjusted the angle of the ambulance, and proceeded to make more roads and driveways next to imaginary houses miles away.

"You gonna do that every time we plays?" Stevie asked without looking up.

Will ignored his best friend's question. "Jus' don't mess up the grader, will ya."

"Okay, b'y. Wanna make a pond?" There was a small stream nearby which they sometimes used to simulate rain, rivers, floods, and other water features of the town, depending on their moods.

"Naw, I'm gonna make a street like I seen on *Adam-12* the other night." He reached for more cop cars to make the scene.

"Okay."

They played in silence in different neighbourhoods for a while. The silence was broken when there was a metallic clink and Stevie stopped moving and said, "Shit."

"What."

Stevie paused, his back to Will. "Man, I didn't mean to."

Will was on his feet. "Let me see."

Stevie handed the body of the grader to his friend, then handed him the grader blade. Stevie knew what the dinky meant to his buddy.

Will turned the pieces over in his hand. The miniature weld that his father, a heavy equipment operator, had done to mend the previous break three years ago had finally given way. Had to happen. There wasn't much surface area to attach, and Stevie was a vigourous road builder.

The repaired grader was the last gift of any consequence Will's father had given him before he wrecked his brand new 1970 Chevelle three days later. An amateur gearhead, he had downed several beers and shots of Screech at the Legion before he decided to show the gathered locals — all four of them, counting Earl the bartender — how cool it sounded and fast it could go. He failed to brake after the stretch and flew off the road on Post Office Turn. That Chevelle was red.

"Stupid bastard," Will muttered.

"What?" Stevie asked.

"Nudding." Will said. "Forget it."

"Sorry, b'y." Stevie said. "You can have my dump truck if you wants. For keeps."

Will tossed the grader and the blade on the Rockpile. He looked at it for a second, then knelt over the accident scene. "That's all right, b'y. Pitch me the backdigger."

"Sure?" Stevie asked, unconvinced.

"Yes, I said!" Will was kneeling over the scene of the accident. A tow truck hauled the mangled Chevelle away to the landfill, and the onlookers dispersed. The ambulance drove away, as did the police cars, without lights or sirens. The Fairlane turned around towards home. A construction crew straightened out the road, eliminating the deadly turn.

"Gettin' too old for dinks anyway," Will said under his breath.

*****

*ED TURPIN is a St. John's resident, but a native of the Burin Peninsula. He is a business analyst with a BA in history and several professional designations. He has well over 20 years' experience in the insurance industry. At last check, he is married with two kids, and enjoys reading and writing in his spare time, even though he doesn't have much of it.*

# Recycling

## By Ed Turpin

The gulls that once noisily clouded the air above the landfill had reduced dramatically since the renovations. One time going to the dump meant you drove through the garbage on temporary dirt paths — not really roads — with your windows up to keep out the stink and the flies. You drove towards a guy wrapped up like someone in a nuclear fallout zone who directed you to the dumping area. You stopped, took a breath, held it, and jumped out of your vehicle to pitch whatever refuse you had as quickly as possible onto a pile. Then you hopped back into your vehicle, exhaled, and rattled and bumped your way back to the road.

Now, you lined up on a paved lot as if waiting to board the ferry to North Sydney. Still a few gulls around, but mainly in the distance, out over the garbage. Nothing to pick at here. Will leaned against the open door of the dumpster, and looked past the garbage horizon out to the blue sea beyond Robin Hood Bay. He was pretty sure this setup was better, but he wasn't convinced. He made a feeble kick at a piece of wood with a nail in it.

Today, on this sunny Saturday morning in May, the spring cleaners were queued five across and seven or eight deep. Not the licensed garbage removal crowd, but the fellas with the SUVs and utility trailers loaded with the wreckage of the winter they had just cleaned up. He told a guy in a Land Rover to put his blue bags in his dumpster and take his household garbage to dumpster number eight on the right and to make sure he had no glass and metals. Same spiel, different audience.

"Arsehole," Will muttered.

"What's with you today?" asked his friend and dumpster partner, Stevie, without looking up.

"Nudding," Will responded curtly.

Will was in his 18th year at the landfill. He had seen a lot in that time. At one time, he was the guy in the hazmat outfit, sweating his arse off pointing dingbats in Cavaliers with soiled mattresses bungeed to the roof of their shitboxes in the right direction. More than once he felt like telling them to drive over the edge of the cliff.

Now, it was different. Much cleaner, less odourous. Cushy, almost. In relative terms, anyway. Now, he took the bags of cans and cardboard and paper and plastic bottles and threw them in the proper pile. Resigned to his station in life, he did his job dutifully and went home every day to his now-empty apartment.

"Sheila, right?" Stevie stood up and stared at him.

"Shut the hell up, will ya?" Will replied.

Stevie shut up. He knew when his friend was crooked.

"Uh, oh," Stevie said a moment later, looking past Will.

Will turned and saw the white Escalade with the Red Sox license plate coming toward their station. His face darkened. The driver saw him, braked, and realized that he had nowhere to go. No going back. He proceeded to the dumpster, and rolled down the window.

"Will," said the driver. "Didn't know you worked Saturdays."

"New schedule," Will snorted.

"Listen ...," the driver began.

Will cut him off. "Containers in number one, cardboard and paper in number two."

The driver said, "Will ..."

This time Stevie cut him off. "I'd dump and run if I was you." He glared at the driver.

The driver dropped his head, sighed, and got out of the giant SUV. He placed his bags in each dumpster as directed. He stopped as if to say something, and then sighed again. He got back into the vehicle and drove off.

Later in the morning, there was a lull. "I'm havin' a pick," Stevie said.

"Go mad," Will muttered as he lit a cigarette.

Stevie kicked around a few blue bags until he saw one that had more legal and letter-sized paper than cereal boxes and toilet paper rolls. He ripped it open and picked through its contents; some power bills for Mrs. Maher on Shaw Street, a Janeway telethon reminder, part of a political science essay. He skimmed through it and wondered who gave a crap about Karl Marx and tossed it over his shoulder. Another bag: insurance renewal documents for Mr. Price in Torbay and some handwritten recipes. Birthday cards. He pocketed a sheet of Peter's Pizza coupons that were still valid.

Another bag: some shredding, but some intact stuff. Discarded fantasy baseball pool statistics, and handwritten player notes. "Hardcore fan," thought Stevie. Some adopt-a-child-in-Africa letters and printed emails. Stevie scanned a few and saw one that referenced Will's cabin in Mahers in the Subject line. Another one mentioned a new Cadillac, and moose hunting. "Uh oh," he said out loud, involuntarily. He looked up and immediately cursed his reflexes.

"What?" said Will, turning.

Stevie tried to hide his findings behind his back. "Uhhhh ... nudding, b'y."

"Give." Will had his hand out.

Stevie knew better than to bother resisting. He handed the papers to Will. He thumbed through them until a couple of keywords jumped out at him on an email. " ... directions ...," " ... cabin in Mahers ...," " ... Will ...," "ME," and "soxcaddy101@xmail.com." Will had seen that email address somewhere before, maybe on Sheila's cellphone, and he knew she always signed her emails "ME." The dates of the emails coincided with his hunting trip to the Northern Peninsula last fall, when Sheila said she was going to her sister's place in Terra Nova. More emails. More plans and schemes to meet and plan a new life and more lies exposed. The dates she referenced in her leaving speech now didn't match so she was lying about how long it had been going on before she decided to leave.

Will and Stevie usually had a good laugh at some of the stuff they found when picking through the bags. The rise of identity theft and the advent of personal shredders reduced their fodder somewhat, but they still had lots of material to mock. This time, however, he was the subject matter, and it wasn't funny.

This was a truth he knew in his heart and was now forced to admit: there was more to the breakup than what he was told. But, it was months ago and there was no going back. He knew that. In some strange way, this confirmation actually steeled his resolve to move on, something he had been working on lately, having only an occasional relapse. He thought he now felt better.

He turned to face Stevie, and smiled weakly. "Who'da thought we'd be pickin' through stuff about ourselves, hey?"

"Sorry, b'y."

"No problem."

"Wanna have a pick?"

"P'raps later."

"Will?"

"What."

"Look." Stevie gestured over his shoulder toward the roundabout. The Escalade driver was out of his vehicle, prying a piece of wood with a nail in it out of the wall of his flat tire on the passenger side.

"You never ..."

"Sorry, b'y."

"Don't be."

"Couldn't resist."

The flow of cars resumed, and they got back to work. As Will tossed containers in number one, and cardboard and paper in number two, Stevie thought he saw a hint of a smile on his friend's face.

# Undertow

## By Keith Collier

One Friday night we had to help Eddie into his car, and he drove it into the end of the bridge down by the farm. I remember the radiator fluid sprayed over the road, the headlights shining down into the water. We had given up trying to convince him not to drive, or offering him a bed for the night. We had to help him out of his car, too, blood running down his face from where his head hit the windshield, and I suppose we should have done something.

But of course we never did, and Eddie kept right on driving. In the winter sometimes he'd take his ATV to the bar, across the ice, avoiding the cops. Summer nights Eddie would sometimes take his boat instead, pulling it up on the beach next to the empty shipbuilding cradles. At closing time we'd help him shove off, stumbling and laughing at the water's edge, and watch him head for home, fighting against the current.

And that current was damn strong. The radio called it a force of nature. In a big speech before the whole town, Smallwood said the same thing, talked about harnessing the watershed, about the dams we were going to build and the pipes and the surge tanks and the turbines that would not only light half the island but turn our bay into a hive of industrial activity. His words, and he was half right, I guess. I was down on the wharf when the boat brought in the huge turbines, and I remember how the flatbed trucks blew out their tires under the weight.

I was 15 then, still a year too young to get a job on the Hydro project. Of course, Eddie helped build the roads, working with the Highways, clearing the survey lines for the heavy equipment that would tear the ground level, dump the crushed stone and lay the asphalt a hundred miles cross-country to the Trans-Canada Highway, just completed the year before. Finish the drive in '65 — another of Smallwood's sayings.

Twenty years later Eddie's son travelled over the same asphalt, heading for Gander and a westbound Air Canada flight. A few years after that the ambulance carrying Eddie's dying wife took the same road out, Eddie hunched in the back while the paramedic went through the motions.

Everybody was proud of the road, our link to civilization — Smallwood again, the man only spoke in catch phrases — but I don't think anybody ever considered the fact that, for all the road would bring into the bay, it would carry people out as well. My own son, pulling out of the driveway in his old Ford Tempo, garbage bags in the backseat stuffed full of clothes.

My father worked 20 years in the lumber woods, cutting pulpwood for Bowater's, running a sawmill, just an old engine block hooked up to a big saw blade next to a small cabin, and I don't think the idea of leaving even occurred to him. He kept it up for 10 years after the Hydro project started. People were building houses with their steady Hydro paycheques, and my father did well, sawing spruce and pine into two-by-fours and rough floor planking, and he took a company job as a cook. For years afterward I'd notice him carefully examining someone's floor or the exposed studs of their basement, checking the grain in the wood as if it still bore his fingerprints.

After that second dam was finished they brought turbines three and four online, and the tailrace current got so strong that it kept the bay from freezing over properly. Out beyond the headlands there would be patches of open water, slush and yellow ice.

The night Eddie died was a cold night at the end of February, and everybody assumed he didn't see the open water because he was drunk, just drove his ATV right into it. I think he just plain forgot that the bay didn't freeze anymore, forgot that this wasn't the same water he had grown up on.

We were at the bar that night, drinking rum and Cokes, nursing beer, playing darts, shooting pool. Eddie had just gotten a big cheque from the Department of Forestry for helping fight a forest fire last summer, and he bought a few rounds and talked about getting a new truck. When the bar closed we saw him down to the edge of the ice, watched as the red taillight of his ATV grew dimmer in the distance and then disappeared around the point. I wonder now if that really was him disappearing around the point, or if we all watched Eddie die without realizing what we were seeing.

The RCMP searched for a few days, but nobody expected to find him, not in that current. The Coast Guard actually found his ATV in the spring, 30 miles away, almost in the open ocean. Carried along by the current, floating upside down from the buoyant tires.

Eddie was a logger, a boat-builder, sometimes a government employee, sometimes a fisherman. He could repair anything mechanical, and collected broken snowmobiles and lawnmowers and chainsaws like some people collect hockey cards. He made a living, a life, here in the bay. But the Hydro project changed it, and this world of mechanical engineers and steady paycheques and helicopters was something Eddie could never really understand.

I know what going through the ice feels like, the shock of icy water and the numbness that comes so fast your fingers are stiff before you even realize you're wet. The pain that comes soon after. On winter nights I can see the current still rippling out there beyond the headlands, beyond the ice, and I try to imagine what Eddie felt as that current pulled him under. I wonder could he still see the streetlights, distant and blurred through the frozen water.

Somewhere back there, through the turbines, the surge tanks, the pipes, and behind the concrete dams I imagine my father's sawmill is still there, the abandoned equipment rusting underwater, the cabin standing exactly as it was when the water came pouring through the trees, creeping up the threshold and the windowpanes and past the tin chimney to the level of the treetops.

Of course, everybody's got fancy cabins on the new shoreline now, propane refrigerators and satellite dishes. Waterskiing on the reservoir, fishing for trout they can't eat because of the mercury.

But damn it if their outboard motors on their boats don't get ruined by those dead trees now and then, still standing there just beneath the surface. I imagine they'll be there for the next hundred years.

*****

KEITH COLLIER grew up in Bay D'Espoir and moved to St. John's to attend Memorial University. He worked at the Railway Coastal Museum, completed an MA and now works as a writer for the Heritage NL website. He is a frequent contributor to the Newfoundland Quarterly and to several collections.

# Listen to the Wolf

## By Owen Whelan

Ralph's daughter called me after the service.

"We're going to take care of his remains later on in the summer," she said. "When everyone's home. He wanted you to help us."

"He's being cremated?"

"That's what he wanted."

"Did he tell you why he wanted me?"

"Something about the two of you and a wolf. Whenever he had a decision to make he'd say, 'Let me listen to the wolf.'"

"That was 50 years ago."

"Dad never talked much, unless he had to. When we asked what he meant, he'd say, 'You had to be there.'"

Over a hot July day an old wolf, the last of his pack, driven by some end-of-life instinct, began a lonely walk down through a Labrador valley to the place of his birth. As he staggered along he remembered the land as it had been: endless forest spread out from the river, lime green caribou moss on the riverbanks, birds and small animals sharing the berries and seeds. He remembered the large caribou herds that moved with the swarms of blackflies across the land, and he remembered the humans who shared his valley. In a short while everything changed. The forest had disappeared, the rivers and lakes were now cloudy, the moss carpet was gone, the caribou were no more and some of the hills had been blasted away. Only the swarms of blackflies remained.

The sun sank slowly as Ralph and I checked building materials in a warehouse yard on the site of a new mining town. For me this was part of a summer job; for Ralph, maybe the beginning of a new career. He'd been offered a permanent position in the new town, and would have to move permanently from his cove on the island. He sometimes spoke about it. I tried to be impartial.

"Can you live the rest of your life feeling you want to be somewhere else? Or will this place grow on you?"

"I don't know," he said.

"You have until Friday. I supposed you could take it, see how it works out. Nothing is permanent."

"I guess that's the way to go."

I made notes on a clipboard as we moved through piles of lumber, Ralph calling information to me. I climbed onto a pile of plywood so I could better see and hear him; my vantage point also let me see down the road towards the town. Ralph called some numbers but my attention was divided between two scenes: him moving through the rows of lumber, sometimes visible and sometimes not, and two men moving along the road towards us, one holding what looked to be a rifle. From his vantage point Ralph could not see them. I watched them check a culvert from both ends, and move closer and closer.

"Two Mounties," I said. "Searching for something — both sides of the road."

Then I saw their quarry. A large wolf came out of the roadside ditch and in among the piles of lumber. Within seconds the wolf and Ralph were face to face. The police were within hearing, but I couldn't shout. I felt stuck to my place for what seemed a long time, while Ralph and the wolf appeared to me as one unit, communicating with each other. The police came on slowly. One of them saw the wolf, raised his rifle in a slow careful motion, and fired. The wolf lifted a little and fell to the side.

I jumped from my perch and reached the wolf with the police; they kept me away while they checked it; there was no need for a second shot. I helped one of them slide the carcass onto a plywood sheet while the other went for their truck. Ralph had disappeared from the yard.

In the evening I went by the detachment where the wolf was on display; the Mounties told the onlookers, including Ralph, that the wolf would be tested, skinned, and probably end up as a trophy at the Company office in Montreal.

"You were there," someone said to me. "Why did they shoot him?"

"Your guess is as good as mine."

"He frightened some of the youngsters in the town-site," someone answered.

"God-damned wolves," another fellow said.

The next morning I went about my routine of lighting a large trash burner and dumping in garbage that had collected overnight. I moved some scrap out of the way of any trucks or forklifts moving by. Ralph met me by the burner.

"I'm going to recommend you for the job they offered me," he said.

"No need. I'm leaving here soon. What made up your mind for you?"

"Open the burner."

I did. And a dead wolf was in there looking out at me.

I had questions: what … how … when … "You'll be hung," I said. "How did you get it?"

"Never mind."

During the next half-hour or so, while Ralph kept workers occupied away from my area, I packed cardboard, wood and shingles around the wolf and sprayed it all with chainsaw gas. When the fire was going well I went to the warehouse office, where Ralph was alone.

"Are you going to tell me why we're doing this?"

"I'm not sure myself. I know you'll laugh, but the wolf charmed me. Put me in a trance."

"I'm not laughing. You were face to face a long time. What was his message?"

"This is not my place."

"It's his? And you want to keep him here?"

It took careful burning to get the wolf into manageable pieces: large bones, ashes and skull. In the following days Ralph spread the remains at what he thought were the wolf's favourite places: on the hilltop near the tower, at the caribou crossing, and along the riverbank. Soon he had only the skull. I suggested he might want a souvenir.

"He stays here. I'll find a place."

On a Sunday morning he found it. At a town church under construction, there was just enough space among the stones of the wall for the wolf skull to sit, unseen, above anyone passing through the doors. Ralph went back to his cove for good a few days later.

On a summer afternoon, Ralph's offspring hear the wolf story for the first time. Then his daughter turns everyone's attention to the job at hand.

"What were his favourite places?"

The others answer as one: "Up the river near the mill ... the old house ... the bakeapple marsh ... out the shore by the light."

"The hilltop," the daughter adds. "He liked to go up there and look out the bay."

I decide to join her and Ralph's granddaughter on the hill. They say a prayer and the young girl empties her small container into a rock crevice at the very top. I take from my pocket two large, yellowed canine teeth and give one to each of them. Their looks question me.

"I just wasn't so pure," I say.

Then they both drop the last of the wolf down among Ralph's ashes.

"Thanks for coming," the daughter says. Then, after a pause, "Did you really believe his wolf story?"

"One hundred per cent," I say. "I was there."

*****

*OWEN WHELAN, originally from Riverhead, St. Mary's Bay, is a writer/painter living in St. John's.*

# Growing things

## By Vicki Combden Murphy

The usual double-stomp of rubber boots on the front deck, the whine of the screen door, then in he burst, bucket in hand, eyes wide with childhood. He was beseeching us to guess before he was halfway in the house, his first word lost in the flowerbed.

"... how many I got t'day!"

I could hear them knocking around in the salt beef bucket, like billiard balls rumbling in the belly of a pool table. Potatoes. Maybe seven or eight. Tiny and pitiful and good enough for him.

"Five!"

Five reasons to not wait for anyone's guess.

His thumb was not green but grey with the smudgery of sonnets and sermons. But potatoes were another form of poetry, willed from dead space with sheer enthusiasm. His hands were meant to turn pages, not soil, nor fat cod drying on Fogo flakes. At 16, he boarded the ferry — to grow his vocabulary, a family, and a scattered stunted spud on a less isolated patch of land.

We were both growing things now. Me, a baby. Him, a tumour. Both feeding off our bodies, getting bigger and stronger and ready to ruin everything. I hurled deals into the great beyond — take this, let me keep that. But I kept getting rounder, which I took as a big fat forget-about-it.

A grapefruit had been growing in Dad's bowel for 10, maybe 20 years. The unluckiest kind of cancer: the one with no symptoms until it has its own postal code. The day they cut it out was the day I saw its replacement — wiggling around on the screen like an upside-down beetle. Three inches of terrible timing.

One soul would be coming in stage left, the other going out stage right. Would they cross paths, brush shoulders, share the stage long enough to sprout something forgettable? Or would they pass like dandelion snow on the wind, miss one another by a breath that may as well be a lifetime because, either way, they're strangers? For nine months I waddled around and wondered, trying to believe in miracles, occasionally pondering what would happen to the order of things to come if I threw myself down the stairs.

I was a prize pumpkin perched on the edge of Dad's bed when the doctor said the second surgery was a flop. The only hope for a cure, flushed away with my mucus plug. The young surgeon said he still had hope, but I could smell a rotting plum down the hall and the stench of bullshit in his every word. The news was a rusty trowel in my gut all the way to China. Dad just stared out the window, smiling at the crocuses poking through the patchy March snow.

That night, I lay in a tub of scalding water, silent and numb, a giant earthworm making waves beneath the taut skin of my belly, trying to remind me I was still alive.

Dad's stitches were closing around his decaying liver, and my eight-pound mass was ready for harvest. But nine days past my due date, I was still holding him in, making time stand still, delaying this and whatever else was about to rock my world. We'd all live off this hope, this little black and white ultrasound picture in my purse. It'd be Christmas Eve forever, the anticipation of good things bringing more joy than their arrival and the sinking knowledge that it'll all soon be over.

By Day 10, I was overthrown by the sheer animal urge to bear down. And then there he was: the living, breathing proof that time had passed, things had grown, change was upon us. He was sucking vigorously on the air, searching blindly for my breast. He had just broken my vagina, now he wanted another piece of me? Fast-forward a few months and he'd be laughing hysterically as they lower my father into the ground. Demon child.

"Would you like him on your breast, mommy?"

"Fuck no."

He found his home in the hollow of Poppy's chest where I spent many a morning reading storybooks to the bass drum of his heart. Both their faces: perfect calm. Like they knew something nobody else did. The moment swept me away, then dragged me back to earth with a crushing smack of irony: here is the man I will bury, holding the boy who will bury me. Less than an inch of flesh and flannel lay between brand new and irreparably broken. There was a fucked-up beauty in it; I see it now. The meaning of life, colliding in a little blue blanket.

The summer sun let us forget if not heal. Inside, organs were quietly packing it in, ready to call it a life. Outside, we pretended we would all live forever. We danced around the cancer, almost thankful for the bastard because at least we had fair warning. A neighbour had dropped dead with a massive heart attack, lying on the floor in a pool of things left unsaid.

Dad grew strawberries, small and pale but sweet. And I grew to love my child, our distraction from the truth, our one perfect thing. Dirty diapers, ceaseless crying, sleepless nights: it was pure joy because it wasn't grief.

The leaves were falling faster now and the sands in the hourglass followed suit, swishing through the tiny canal like the beach was finally calling them home. But Dad was slowing down, the pain in his side making it difficult for him to walk. He took his meals on the couch with a dishtowel on his chest for a bib, the checkered cloth enabling a feeble game of peek-a-boo, the boy pulling himself up from the floor to pull away the rag.

"Boo."

Each time, Poppy was still there, to both of our surprise.

The slanted garden sank into a morphine slumber, crab grass filling in the spaces like it was never there. I collected his poems in a banana box; the colour of the paper whispered the age of each piece — from parched sunflower gold to new lily white.

A green, die-cast train comes to a halt at the base of the casket, a boy crawling after it, grunting with glee. Four feet above him dad's hands are folded upon one another. They look odd without a book, or a pen, or a bucket of something plucked from the earth. His face is sunken and clay-like and not his own, but he is surrounded by his favourite things so I know it's him: books, flowers, trees at each corner of his casket in rich forest green, and people — their faces proud and kind and resilient. I imagine the casket brimming with tiny potatoes, their gnarly eyes following me around the floral wall-papered room.

I pick up my boy who chortles at the sight, blissfully oblivious to the colossal shift that has just occurred beneath my feet. There he is and here he is, the bookends of my existence. I stand, sad but sturdy, lost but lucky. Firmly rooted in my father's earth, I stretch toward the sun.

*****

*VICKI COMBDEN MURPHY is a mother, wife and writer from Badger's Quay, now living in Torbay. She works in creative direction at m5 where she started as a writer over 11 years ago. She is the author of motherblogger.ca where she chronicles her adventures in Toddlerville.*

Pam Frampton is associate managing editor and a columnist with The Telegram. She has a BA (Honours) in English literature from Memorial University of Newfoundland and has worked as a journalist for more than 20 years. Originally from Trinity Bay, she lives in St. John's with her husband, videojournalist Glenn Payette, and their grey furry, four-legged son. She is also the editor of Volumes I, II and III of *The Cuffer Anthology*.